Sherlock Holmes and the Egyptian Tomb Mystery

By Joanna M. Rieke

Paperback ISBN 978-1-78705-693-0
Epub ISBN 978-1-78705-694-7
PDF ISBN 978-1-78705-695-4

MX Publishing, 335 Princess Park Manor, Royal Drive,
London, N11 3GX
www.mxpublishing.com

Cover design by Brian Belanger
Translation by Bryan Stone

Dedicated to Helen, Susan and Thomas, who have warmly
welcomed me into their Swiss family

221B Baker Street

The year 1890 had begun quietly. In April, however, as the reader will no doubt recall, there occurred a series of gruesome murders, which set the people of London in alarm. There seemed to be no common features apart from the brutal way in which death had come to the victims. The affair achieved notoriety as the "Thames Murders," since all the dead were found near the river in east London. I had the honour to help Holmes in his enquiries, and I saw how all his faculties and intellectual gifts were challenged. In this task, the first time I could again work with him after my marriage, we found our lives endangered by unscrupulous villains who could, thankfully, be brought to their deserved punishment. We did not escape unscathed, both of us being wounded. While Holmes returned from hospital to his Baker Street rooms, I was invited to take a few days' convalescence, accompanied by my dear wife, Mary, in Robertsbridge, a sleepy village in east Sussex, where Mary's good friend Mrs. Forrester had her country house. I made a good recovery, which was as well, since it became apparent that, even in this rural scene, there were around us criminal activities which took on ominous and frightening aspects. Holmes was not unaware, and came from London to find a dramatic adventure whose outcome was up to the last on a knife-edge. What we called the *'Secret of the Three Monks'* was an evil plot, which he was able at last to foil, and so to bring events to a conclusion.

Holmes then returned to Baker Street while Mary and I enjoyed what remained of our Robertsbridge holiday. My return was, however, soon pressing, for I could not impose indefinitely on my neighbour, Dr. Smythe, who was kindly looking after my practice in Kensington. Indeed, when I returned home there was plenty of work for me to address. I was quickly caught up in my daily affairs, mornings being for consultations and afternoons for house visits. My free time, often rare, I naturally spent with Mary. I had however resolved to visit Holmes as soon as possible, and on August 1st, the opportunity presented itself. My appointments required that I only make one visit that day, and so it was early afternoon when I arrived at 221B Baker Street.

Mrs. Hudson greeted me in almost motherly style, and asked in detail about Mary and myself. I had of course to satisfy her feminine curiosity, before I could take the familiar stairway to our rooms above. I hesitated and then knocked, for Mrs. Hudson had assured me that Holmes was there. I waited, expecting him to invite me in, but nothing happened. Carefully I turned the doorknob and opened the door a crack. There, in that room which was so familiar to me, was Holmes, in his favourite armchair, by the fireplace, with his knees drawn up. His eyes were set upon a gold watch, which he held in one hand. He appeared quite immersed in his thoughts and unaware of his surroundings. "Holmes?" I asked quietly, taking a few steps into the room.

At once his eyes opened wide, as if he had been deeply sleeping. He turned to me, and there appeared for a moment a fleeting smile on his lips. Then he leapt out of the armchair, allowed the watch, which he had been examining, to slide gently onto the table and stepped briskly toward me, to shake my hand vigorously.

"My dear Watson, it is so good to see you here again. I hope you are now fully recovered from our adventure in Robertsbridge?"

"Thank you, Holmes, I think now fully. And how are you?"

"Very well", and then he continued after a short pause, "But at present I have no case on which I can work."

Concerned and somewhat alarmed, I looked at Holmes, but before I could go further into what was troubling me, Holmes answered the question forming within me.

"Please don't be alarmed, Watson. I have not had to have recourse to my seven-per-cent solution. My days were very adequately filled with a number of chemical experiments, and with the completion of *'The classification of products of combustion,'* my new monograph.*"

I was surprised that my friend had so readily answered a question that I had not yet posed, and I looked curiously at him, but he continued without a moment's pause.

"It was not difficult to follow your thoughts, old friend. As I said that I have no case before me at this time, your regard became apparent at once, and somewhat suspiciously, your eyes swept over my desk, where as you knew, I always keep my needles and the seven-per-cent solution. You then looked back at me, but this was not the regard of a friend; rather was it of a critical and analytical doctor, looking for symptoms. What other matter could have concerned you so much as that which I had deduced?"

I was once more impressed by Holmes' ability to observe and reason. Before I could dwell further on this, however, he had already changed the subject, and asked me if I were in a hurry, or could I spend a little time with him. I told him that the rest of the day was my own. I saw how a satisfied smile came over his features.

We were soon comfortably settled in our familiar places by the fireplace. We poured ourselves a sherry, and prepared to smoke, while Holmes asked me about Mary and about the practice in Kensington. Although he was obviously listening carefully to me, I noticed that he could not resist a glance at the gold pocket watch which he had left on the table as I came in. I resolved to ask him about it.

"That is an unusual looking watch there on the table, Holmes. How do you come to have it?"

I saw how a smile came again to his lips, and his eyes lit up. It was quite clear that he was pleased that our conversation could now move to a subject which might be important to him.

"It is indeed an unusual piece, Watson. May I invite you to look at it more closely?" With these words, he picked up the watch, to hand it to me. He then added "It belongs to an elderly gentleman who called this morning in the hope of seeing me. Mrs. Hudson saw that he was in a very nervous state, but unfortunately I was at the Diogenes Club."

Upon hearing that, I broke off my examination of the watch, to look straight back at Holmes. The Diogenes Club, with its strict rules to protect the privacy of each of its members, is perhaps the most unusual of all the clubs in Her Majesty's realm. The members have no contact with one another, and conversations take place only in the Strangers' Room. And of all the members, surely the most remarkable is Holmes' older brother, Mycroft. I well recall how I first met him there in the Strangers' Room.

Mycroft's intelligence is in no way inferior to that of his younger brother Sherlock, but in all other respects the two are very different. While Mycroft Holmes lives quietly, and almost exclusively, in Pall Mall or at the Diogenes Club, one must describe Sherlock Holmes' life as erratic and adventurous. These thoughts occupied my mind as Holmes continued his remarks.

"Yes, Watson, you have surmised correctly. I was visiting my brother Mycroft. He had called upon me in order to hear my opinion on a particularly vexatious matter. As you are aware, Watson, Mycroft not only works for the government. In many ways it would be better to say that Mycroft *is* The Government, for many of the issues which Mycroft is called upon to resolve are difficult affairs, and at the highest level. But I am very conscious of your loyalty, honour and discretion, and feel I can safely involve you in the affair. Would the matter interest you?"

"Thank you for your confidence, Holmes; I would be honoured to learn more."

"Then, Watson, listen carefully. For nearly two years, under the Treaty of Constantinople of 29 October. 1888, Great Britain has accepted the Protectorate of the Suez Canal. The canal, as you know, connects the Mediterranean with the Red Sea, and has for British interests a high strategic importance. Now on our main trading route with India, it avoids that ships are forced to round the Cape of Good Hope. The trade route to India is shortened by a quarter, and the passage is much safer by way of the Canal. In order to be aware of the full implications of its Protectorate role, Her Majesty's government decreed that plans should be drawn up showing potentially vulnerable situations, and points where attacks might be attempted. This has been a lengthy task, carried out in full secrecy, and was only completed a month ago. You will readily imagine, Watson, what it might mean to potential enemies, especially Germany and the Austro-Hungarian Empire, if they could possess such sensitive plans. After completion, the documents were lodged in a safe at the British Embassy in Cairo.

As we have however learned, this was not enough to assure their safety. They disappeared from the safe. The senior officer, Edward Parker, was in a position to take possession of the papers. When the loss was observed, suspicion fell at once on Parker, as he was the only person authorised to have sole access, for normal business purposes, to the safe. There was no doubt, the more so because he resisted arrest, and in doing so he was fatally injured. There was now no way in which he could tell us for whom he had stolen the papers. This regrettable story is bad enough, but there is worse to come. Neither on his person, nor in his private rooms, was there any trace of the papers or of those for whom he had removed them." Holmes paused to draw thoughtfully on his pipe, and I waited in alarm upon the rest of his account. "The failure to maintain security at the Embassy was now followed by an intensive control at all the frontier points, but all was in vain; the papers remained lost."

"My goodness, Holmes. But how might you be able to help? The secret papers could be anywhere, and might still be in Cairo or elsewhere in Egypt. Are you being asked to conduct enquiries in London, far from the scene, or is Mycroft hoping to send you to Cairo to investigate there?"

Holmes laughed and added, "You are quite right, Watson. Here in London I can contribute little, and in Cairo, the scent is no longer warm. Mycroft knows this well, but he had called me, because something unusual did come to light as Parker's body was examined. In his mouth was a scrap of paper on which the following letters had been written." And he took up a narrow strip of paper, dirty and yellow, on which the following letters could be read.

GPSDLA LSWIA RLTI CIVPT E NFH EEOMR1 IA R I 2E

It said nothing to me, and I looked at him thoughtfully. "It is presumably a fragment of an incriminating message," he suggested. "As Parker realised that he was trapped, he must have torn it to shreds and tried to swallow in. He did not quite succeed, before the fatal shot killed him, and this was left."

"It's a pity that no more was left of this paper, Holmes".

"That is what I said to Mycroft. It is not possible, with this fragment and with no other help, to reach any useful conclusions. No, I regret that this paper and these few characters are useless. They cannot serve to draw any conclusions." With this he picked it up, crushed it and threw it into the cold fireplace, to lie with other scraps that he had thrown there earlier.

"This watch tells us much more. What do you make of it, Watson? Have you already formed an opinion on the owner?"

"I think I have, Holmes. The watch is of a large diameter, and the chain attached to it is at least twenty-four inches long, rather than the usual eighteen. That points me towards ostentation, which as we know often goes together with doubtful taste. That is also shown by the heavy clasp on the chain, and also the conspicuously plain dial. The engravings on both sides of the cover are certainly well executed, but very unusual. That on the front shows a great eye, a certain proof that the owner is a Freemason, and on the back is the Latin motto, *Dominus Illuminator Mea,* which means, God is my light. That may mean a certain curious form of belief, such as is not unusual in Freemasonry circles. Summing up, I am led to suggest that the owner, your visitor of this morning, comes from a humble background, is relatively uneducated, and may, perhaps through marriage, have come into a certain wealth. He has now the means to purchase things which please him, but not the discretion to choose wisely. He belongs to a Freemasonry lodge, and may have a somewhat fanatical religious background."

I broke off and looked expectantly at Holmes. He smiled quietly as he looked back at me and answered. "My dear Watson, I must congratulate you for your gifts of observation. Apart from some small details, you have noted all the significant features which are needed to justify drawing conclusions." Holmes' words naturally pleased me, indeed made me modestly proud, as he was always economical in his praise. My feeling of satisfaction was, however, brief, for he then continued:

"Regrettably, all the conclusions you have reached are incorrect." I looked up rather irritated, but he carried on, without taking any notice of me, to explain what he thought.

"I will take each individual feature in turn, so that you can understand why you were mistaken.

1. The size of the watch, the clear dial, and the long chain with the heavy clasp, speak unmistakeably for an owner who suffers from poor eyesight.
2. The inscription on the back is taken from the 27th Psalm, verse 1. This is the heraldic motto of the University of Oxford.

3. The engraving on the front is a representation of an Egyptian hieroglyph. This subject is better known as the eye of Horus. In Egyptian mythology, Seth, the god of the desert, fights with Horus for the throne of Osiris, the god of the Underworld, and tears out his eye. Thot, the wise god of the moon, restores the eye of Horus, with the result that the eye of Horus is also referred to as the Udiat-Eye, since udiat means intact, complete or healthy."

I had not intended to interrupt Holmes in this explanation, but his long excursion into Egyptian mythology, which for me was a complete mystery, demanded a certain explanation. Before he continued, therefore, I asked him outright: "My goodness, Holmes, what brings you to have such a commanding knowledge of Egyptian mythology? I recall that you have always said that you only retain as much knowledge as you require for your use."

"That is certainly so, Watson, I regard my brain as a storeroom, with only limited space. Only a fool would collect so much that is of no use, leave it lying there and then afterwards no longer find what he really needs. I only collect things I need, and arrange them in such a way that I can at once find what is important. That was the case with my knowledge of Egyptology, which was of the greatest value in the case of the stolen Horus falcon."

As Holmes spoke about this, my interest was immediately awakened anew, for this must have been one of his earlier cases from the time before we met. I hoped that I might hear more about it, but he was already anxious to pick up our earlier subject.

"Before we continue to examine the watch, I should mention that the eye of Horus was often found as a protective charm. But let us continue.

4. If you will open the spring cover on the back, you will see that there where a key should be inserted to wind up the watch, there are a number of scratches. Such scratches are typical of people who are hasty or careless, but also by persons with weak eyesight. Since however there are no scratches on the watchcase itself, we see that the owner has taken care of it.
5. The watch is of interest as a special model produced by the German company Junghans. The arrangement of the gearwheels betrays that it is a model first sold only some two years ago. Only a few were made, and it was very costly. I fear that it was certainly beyond the reach of even a well-paid university lecturer.
6. As I returned to Baker Street, I found the watch lying open on the table. Despite the long chain, which permitted the owner to lift it to eye level, he had detached it from the chain, better to consult it. As he waited, he placed it on the table, where, when he had to depart, he left it. That also suggests poor eyesight. It also confirms Mrs Hudson's observation, that he appeared very nervous. Indeed, if he left behind his watch, he may have been in desperation.

Let me therefore summarise what we have. I suspect that our visitor is a retired professor of archaeology. He was surely long engaged as a lecturer at the University of Oxford, from where he took his retirement some two years ago. On that occasion he received this fine watch, which tells us so much about its owner. This situation may have reflected his age, but certainly also his optical weakness. More than that I cannot say, apart from the obvious fact that our visitor was burdened by a most difficult problem." Quite astonished, I looked at Holmes with curiosity. I could not deny that his conclusions were logical, and yet that seemed in no way a proof that they were in fact correct. I found that my own thoughts could not be dismissed so lightly, and resolved to try again.

"Holmes, that is all very plausible, but are your conclusions not based purely on assumptions?" Just as I said this, there was a knock on the door, and Mrs. Hudson appeared. Holmes looked at her expectantly, and she said: "Mr. Holmes, the gentleman who had hoped to see you this morning is here again. I thought this time to ask for his card."

As she spoke, she handed to Homes a small visiting card. He took it in at a glance, and asked Mrs. Hudson to show in the visitor. As I listened to the steps on the stair, Holmes gave me the visiting card, with an unmistakeable smile on his lips. Again amazed, I read what was printed:

Professor Richard Hammond
Professor of the Faculty of Archaeology
University of Oxford

The Visitor

As our visitor entered, and cautiously asked if he were speaking to Mr. Holmes, my friend took a step towards him, and led him to the sofa near my armchair. I stood up to greet him and Holmes introduced me: "Professor Hammond, this is my friend and colleague, Dr. Watson."

The hand which I took was ivory-coloured and icy cold. My grasp was hardly returned, and the greeting from our visitor could scarcely be understood; it might even be called incoherent. His face was pale, and the effect was reinforced by his white hair. There were beads of perspiration on his upper lip, and on his forehead. His eyes were the only feature which seemed to live, as they flickered around him through a pair of thick, almost grotesque eyeglasses. I really did not need to be a doctor to recognise that this was a man close to a nervous breakdown and perhaps to a dangerous collapse. I looked in alarm to Holmes and said, "Holmes, Professor Hammond urgently needs a large whisky!"

Holmes filled a glass, and I helped Professor Hammond to a lying position on the sofa, at the same time easing the pressure of his collar. I cautiously helped him to sip the whisky, and spoke to him, as far as possible, to calm him. My quiet words and the whisky after a few moments elicited the desired effect; he became less agitated and his features recovered a little colour. As he felt stronger, he sat up and spoke, in obvious embarrassment. "My dear sirs, I am so very sorry that I have burdened you with my weakness. But since last night I have felt myself in a terrible nightmare, from which I am unable to awaken. Mr. Holmes, I need your help!"

Holmes had at first simply observed, with a detached air, the professor's recovery, but now I saw that his concern and interest were being aroused.

"Professor Hammond, as soon as you feel strong enough, I would invite you to explain, as clearly as you can, your problem, leaving nothing out. Every detail may be of interest. If it does not disturb you, Dr. Watson will make notes"

"That will be quite in order" replied Professor Hammond. He looked across, perhaps a little irritated, at Holmes, who sat with his knees drawn up in his armchair, and closed his eyes. But all was well, and so he began, although, as he said, "I really don't quite know where I should start. It is perhaps best if I start a little further in the past".

Holmes gave no sign, so he continued, "As you have seen from my card, my professional concern is archaeology. The humanities had interested me from childhood, especially various cultures. I would greatly have wished to take part in excavations in overseas countries, but my poor eyesight rendered that impossible. I will however make no complaint; I have never regretted my time, over decades, teaching in Oxford. Although it was denied me to have my own family, I found a ready substitute in the respect and friendship of my colleagues and my students. You will thus observe, gentlemen, that it was in my nature to lead an ordered and quiet life.

"My younger brother Archibald, however, was completely the opposite. He went out seeking adventure, and had little time for books and education, although he was without doubt intelligent. His principal preoccupations seemed to be playing cards, drinking, fighting and, well, let us say, superficial romantic attachments. My father tolerated this as long as he could, but it could not continue indefinitely, and there came a day when Archibald and the family had to go separate ways. It will scarcely surprise you that he turned to the Army, and so he was posted in 1857 to India with the Seventeenth Light Dragoons. The regiment landed in December, and was in May 1858 ready for action when the Sepoy mutiny was almost over. Fresh troops were however still required, as companies of bandits continued to make the country insecure. It was at this time that he came to serve with Evelyn Wood, who, as you may know, received the Victoria Cross.

"Military life seemed to give a sense of purpose and structure to Archibald's life. He was promoted to sergeant, and then selected as officer, in time to be in 1873 one of the thirty-five officers of the so-called 'Wolseley Ring.' Their task was, under General Joseph Wolseley, to bring to an end the Ashanti uprising in the African Gold Coast. Following this, with his military service record, and with wounds he had received, he was invited to return to Britain as an invalid, and to take honourable retirement. He chose however to remain in Africa, certainly not least because he had for some years been living with an Arab woman with whom he had a son, named Brian.

I do not know if he had married the woman, but the official papers in my possession show that Brian was his legitimate son. I also know that they lived for some time in Equatoria, the region on the Upper Nile to which Samuel White Baker came in 1870, and which he was to administer in the hope of stopping the slave trade. Archibald had a good position under Baker, in Equatoria; unfortunately, the situation in the Egyptian kingdom was deteriorating. A popular national movement was growing stronger. This was the Urabi movement, followers of the Egyptian officer Ahmad Urabi Pasha, now War Minister.

"You will surely recall that Britain was at first, despite its wide-ranging financial commitment in Egypt, cautious about this. It was only when Urabi Pasha formed his own army, brought the whole of Egypt under his control, and threatened our communications with India through the Suez Canal, that Prime Minister Gladstone decided to intervene. In 1882 British soldiers were sent, and there were some battles. As Brian's mother was now dead, Archibald left the boy with comrades in Equatoria, and again joined General Wolseley, who was marching with an army through the desert in the direction of Cairo. Half-way there, near Tel El-Kebir, Wolseley's troops encountered and defeated the army of Urabi. My brother Archibald, however, could not share in the victory, as he fell in the battle. Brian was now an orphan, and was left as a fourteen-year-old to fend for himself.

"As I learned this, I felt obliged to help my nephew. I paid for his journey to England and gave him a home with me. It was at first not easy, as he hardly understood English. However, he was intelligent and lively, and learned quickly. He had never been to school, so I taught him myself, so that he would have a broad general education. In view of his background, I also taught him something of Egyptology. At first he was simply a good and attentive scholar, but as my eyesight deteriorated, he became more and more my assistant. I had already come to love Brian as if he were my own son.

"Some two years ago, the University suggested I might like to retire. I would have liked to have kept Brian with me at home, but I knew that, with only my own modest savings, this would not be possible. I also realised, however, that it would not be good. I could not bind him to me; he had a right to his own life. Long deliberation, about the kind of work in which he might usefully engage, led to my recalling that Dr. Vincent Miller, the Director of the Egyptian Department of the British Museum, had completed part of his studies with me. I found an occasion to speak to him, and Dr. Miller was only too pleased to engage him as an assistant. Just a year ago, he accompanied Dr. Miller on an excavation in Egypt. Dr. Miller was full of praise for Brian, who not only knew his subject but also spoke perfect Arabic, a great help at the excavation site."

Professor Hammond paused, and I took the opportunity to offer him a fresh whisky. I also looked across at Holmes to see whether, as I feared, this long account had tried his patience. I had no cause for concern. He still sat in his armchair, his knees up, his eyes closed and his finger-tips pressed together. An unprepared observer might think he was not listening, but I knew, from the years as his friend and partner, that his full concentration was fixed on that which Professor Hammond was relating, and now continued.

"It would have seemed that all was going well, but early this week Brian's good fortune took a dramatic blow. He and Dr. Miller had arrived in London on the SS Bokhara, a steamer of the Peninsular and Orient Line, from Alexandria. They had brought with them for the museum a great treasure, the contents of an intact Egyptian burial chamber, a tomb which Dr Miller had excavated. This was indeed the main object of their excavations, and they were authorised to bring all their finds from Egypt for exhibition in London. The unloading and removal to the museum were to take place on Tuesday; Dr. Miller was in attendance at the ship's side. There occurred, however, for reasons not yet clear, a dreadful accident, from which Dr. Miller received fatal injuries. You may have seen the report in 'The Times' the next day."

Prof. Hammond paused and looked towards Holmes, who made no comment but nodded, so that Professor Hammond continued. "It was this accident which brought me at once to London, where I intend to pay my last respects to Dr. Miller, and also to offer what help I can to Brian. My nephew would now again be on his own, and would also have to accompany the completion of the unloading, the formalities and the unpacking of the contents of the tomb, so carefully packed in Egypt by himself and Dr. Miller. I think it was for this reason that he was last night in the cellars of the British Museum.

"It was there that two of the night watchmen found him, with a bloodstained knife in his hand, beside the stabbed body of another watchman."

Professor Hammond paused again, and then took a larger draught from his whisky. Then, with some emotion, he continued, "As soon as I heard, I went to Scotland Yard, where Brian was taken, to talk with him. He refused to see me. Heaven only knows what is in his mind. I learned from his lawyer that he has denied the murder, but gives no explanation of why he was again in the British Museum cellar. I fear that he is in deep trouble, for not only did the other watchmen find him there with the knife, but they also both report that they knew of an argument the day before between Bryan and the same watchman. Please, Mr. Holmes! I implore you to help Brian! Prove that he is innocent, find out the truth!"

He was leaning forward, begging Holmes to help him. Holmes however did not change his position, just as at the start of this account. Indeed, as he answered, he remained as he was.

"My dear professor, I have to say that the evidence against your nephew seems very powerful. I will nevertheless gladly attempt to find any facts there may be, which might change his position. I cannot promise you any success. Please reflect, however, professor, that the truth which I can discover may not be that which you are hoping to hear."

As he finished his reply, there was a heavy silence in the room. But then I was surprised by the voice of Professor Hammond, as he spoke with a clarity and strength which I would not have imagined possible. "Mr. Holmes, I will know the truth! I am personally convinced that Brian cannot have done this, and yet, should he prove to be guilty, I must also know that! Mr. Holmes, please let me have the truth, regardless of what it turns out to be!"

He had scarcely said this, then Holmes opened wide his eyes, jumped up like a tense spring from his armchair, leapt across the room and spoke, in a tone which brooked no contradiction:

"Professor Hammond, I suggest that you go back now to your hotel, and leave everything else to us. Dr Watson will note the details."

With these words, he gave the pocket watch back to the Professor, who looked somewhat overwhelmed already, and went to the door to show him out. I had just time to make my notes and speak some words of encouragement, before Holmes closed the door.

As soon as we were alone, Holmes turned to me beaming and rubbing his hands together in anticipation. He walked several times with long steps energetically up and down the room. Then he stopped, and he looked directly at me.
"How is it with you, old friend, would you like to accompany me once again in my investigations?"

"Indeed I would, Holmes!" "Wonderful", replied Holmes, as he reached out for his hat and stick, and went ahead down the stairs, calling back enthusiastically, "Come on, Watson, the game is afoot".

In the British Museum

Our first call was to the British Museum. It was quite busy, surely a most desirable thing for a museum, but it soon became apparent that the interest of some visitors was less a reflection of their concern for foreign or historic cultures, but more out of sensational curiosity, on account of the murder. It was therefore not a surprise, that the Director of the Museum, Lord Armstrong, although he obviously knew Holmes, displayed no great pleasure in our visit. Holmes quickly made clear to him that the purpose of our visit was to make enquiries which, as we hoped, would support the traditional good reputation of the museum. He now readily agreed, and prepared to accompany us into the cellars, to the scene of the murder.

As so often in such cellars, there was a stuffiness, an almost mildew-like smell in the air. You have, dear reader, surely often been almost overwhelmed in the museum's public exhibition rooms by the number and richness of the exhibits, but I would assure you that it in no way compares with the situation awaiting you in the cellars. The claustrophobic effect is accentuated by the poor lighting. There penetrates from the outside world, through the half-round barred casement windows, only a thin illumination, from the already drab London streets. Gas and oil lamps are completely absent, as the danger of fire is ever present. There are numerous well-protected carbide lamps which give some light, but which seem thereby only to accentuate the shadowy, almost menacing, darkness.

During our tour, Lord Armstrong explained to us the problems facing the Museum's administration, starting with the need for continuous renovation of the building itself. Only in the previous week all windows of the facade had been newly painted. With this came the constant need to ensure that new exhibition material would attract their public. He was obvious greatly concerned with the exhibition, starting the following week, of the contents of a newly discovered Egyptian tomb, a burial chamber, of which he had great hopes. Suddenly, however, he stopped, and stretched out his hand saying, with a subdued voice,

"Here is where we found Watchman Peter Shephard". The spot had been scrubbed, but the stain was still clearly visible, a large dark patch. It was unmistakeably the spot where the watchman's blood had soaked into the stone floor. Holmes took out his magnifying glass, and in a moment he was on the floor, to Lord Armstrong's surprise, on all fours, crawling along. Lord Armstrong looked at me questioningly, but I could only shrug my shoulders, and asked him, "What is stored in all these crates?"

"We have in the cellars all those exhibits which are either not presently being exhibited, or need further research, or are new acquisitions. In this section you see the crates from Egypt, which the unfortunate Dr. Miller had brought for us."

He interrupted here his discourse to reach out with some surprise and pick up two miniature pictures, which to me looked as if they had been carelessly dropped on a box near the bloodstain which Holmes had so carefully studied. More to himself than to me, he muttered, "I am always drawing attention to valuable exhibits which are not properly stored."

He put down the two miniatures again, on the crate, and continued, "With all the disturbance of the murder, we have not even started yet with the unpacking of Dr. Miller's material, but this evening we will do so. Time is short, but the exhibition room is ready, and everything is well documented. We should be finished on Sunday, so that the exhibition can open on Monday, as we have advertised it in 'The Times.' Then we can show to the public our reconstruction of the burial chamber."

It was not difficult to see that Lord Armstrong attached much importance to this new exhibition. Holmes had in the meantime completed his careful and minute study of the floor and also of the crates alongside. There was no way of telling how long he would still need, but for me the narrow space and poor air were becoming rapidly unpleasant. It was clear that Lord Armstrong was also affected, so I asked Holmes if he needed me, as otherwise I could be found in the exhibition room on the first floor. There was no clear answer, but as he grunted and interrupted his muttering to himself, I assumed his agreement and accompanied Lord Armstrong upstairs.

It was a relief to go upstairs, from this oppressive cellar. The exhibition room on the first floor had already been cleared of other material, and prepared for the new exhibition. Great sailcloth sheets hung on the walls, painted with Egyptian pictures, symbols and writing, creating the impression of the interior of the tomb, and there were glass topped display cases, at present empty but waiting to receive the new material. The largest of the glass cabinets had a truly dramatic dimension, towering above us.

Lord Armstrong, who was very occupied with this exhibition, explained with obvious pride, "This glass shrine is a very special construction, Dr. Watson. I think there is nothing like it elsewhere. We will here exhibit the open sarcophagus from the tomb, with the mummy in it." I could only reply that it would surely be a unique exhibition.

I must admit that my first thought was that the dead person who was to be exhibited would perhaps have been more comfortable in his or her appointed tomb in Egypt. From the point of view of scientific learning, however, it was certainly a great benefit, that this mummy could be exhibited here in such conditions, and with the assurance that the dead would here be treated with dignity and respect. That was not always the case among my colleagues in the medical profession, for some of whom it was not unusual to prescribe a powder made from grinding mummified remains in their pestle and mortar.

This, dear reader, may surprise, or even provoke a certain disgust. You may then be even more surprised to know that such powders, derived from mummies, belong to the stock-in-trade of many pharmacists, where they can also be purchased without a prescription. To look for healing and recovery from the remains of the dead, even of such great age, is for me only a superstitious fraud, a disgrace to those of my profession who hold to it. Being reminded of such things had a disturbing effect upon my stomach, so I turned back to Lord Armstrong in an attempt to calm myself. "Lord Armstrong, may I ask whether you have the same passionate interest in all parts of your remarkable collection? Or do you perhaps have a special sympathy for Egyptology?"

Lord Armstrong laughed and said, "I must confirm your suspicion, Dr. Watson, and I see that your partnership with my friend Mr. Holmes has already sharpened your observation! Yes, indeed, Egyptology is my hobby-horse."

Mention of Holmes reminded me that we might now go back to find him. I turned back towards the staircase, whilst Lord Armstrong recounted to me his love of Egyptian archaeology. As he did so, I recalled Holmes' remarks about the Horus falcon, and having still only an imprecise picture of its significance, I took the opportunity to ask him to tell me more. "Why, Dr. Watson, of course! The Horus falcon, in Egyptian mythology, is a particular representation of the god, Horus. It is, as often with myths, presented in various forms. Sometimes the falcon is complete; and sometimes we have a human figure with a falcon's head. Almost always, the falcon's head is shown carrying the royal double crown." I had to ask again, what this might mean.

"Yes, Dr. Watson, you have heard correctly. In the north of Egypt, the Nile delta, we find Lower Egypt. Further south, reaching up the Nile to Aswan, was Upper Egypt. In Upper Egypt the symbols of power were the lotus plant and the so-called white crown. This crown was pear-shaped and on the front it displayed a lotus flower motif, and a vulture goddess, the patron saint of Upper Egypt. In Lower Egypt the symbols of power were the papyrus plant and the red crown. This crown resembled a cap, of which the back pointed sharply upwards. At the front the cap had a point, as high as at the rear, which represented a red papyrus blossom. On the front of the crown was a representation of a snake, the Egyptian cobra, the patron goddess of Lower Egypt. The cobra is shown reared up, ready to strike, as a symbol that the bearer of the crown is always ready to attack any power who comes with evil intent."

I was hearing a quite fascinating account, by an expert.

"The Horus falcon wears both crowns, and thus unites Upper and Lower Egypt. There are many representations of the falcon, both as mural decoration and as sculpture. There seems to have been no limit to the size and materials employed. And then there are the versions as amulets, because the Horus falcon was regarded as a protection for all who carried it."

Lord Armstrong had just concluded this account as we entered the great entrance hall of the Museum. We were surprised to find Holmes there, apparently completely absorbed in thought, looking out of an open window on the façade. As he realised that we were approaching, he hurried over to us and asked Lord Armstrong with some urgency, whether there had been any thefts from the museum in recent weeks. Somewhat surprised, looking up and then answering thoughtfully, he replied, "No, Mr. Holmes, we have had no thefts or break-ins for several months. What makes you ask this?" But Holmes did not seem to have heard the question. Instead, he simply expressed thanks that he had been so kindly received, and Lord Armstrong, obviously still somewhat puzzled, could only say courteously that he was pleased to have been of assistance.

"Dear Lord Armstrong, you were indeed most helpful! And if I may, I will ask you one thing more, might you provide me with the name and address of the dead watchman?"

"But naturally, Mr. Holmes, he lived at 47 Cudworth Street, Whitechapel. It is, as you surely will find, an unsavoury district, but please do not think on that account any the worse of Peter Shephard. He was a fine and upright man, frank and honest, just as one might expect from a former soldier of Her Majesty. He had indeed been an officer in Africa, but with his wound he found no work or support. When I first saw him, he was almost destitute, but still he had dignity. I saw just the character that we needed.

In the fifteen years that he was with us here, he has never found any task too great. He still had a disability, as his leg never recovered from the war wound, and things were surely not always easy for him, but I never heard him complain."

"Thank you again, Lord Armstrong" said Holmes, and turned on his heel to walk away with rapid steps. I was left to take leave of a still somewhat uncertain Lord Armstrong and to thank him properly for his courtesy, before hurrying away to catch up with Holmes in Great Russell Street, where he was already hailing a hansom to go to Cudworth Street.

I had no idea what he had discovered, but the brilliance in his eyes told me that something was occupying him. If I had hoped that he would tell me on the way what he was thinking, I was disappointed. He said not a word about the case, but regaled me with an account of the violin concerto performance which he had recently attended in the Royal Albert Hall.

47, Cudworth Street

During this account, our hansom had covered a considerable distance, and more than simply geographically. We saw a profound change in our surroundings. With every turn of the wheels, the streets were dirtier and the alleyways less inviting. In one of the most uninviting, in the shadow of a long railway viaduct, the cab stopped, and the driver called out that this was Cudworth Street. Holmes asked him to wait, and, to encourage him to do so, promised a half-sovereign over the return fare. With that, we went to find No. 47.

As were all the houses in the street, this was a three-storey brick building, without porch or garden, directly on the pavement. I rang the bell but heard nothing, and nothing happened. I looked at Holmes, and he took his stick to knock sharply three times on the door. There was another pause, but we heard movement inside. Again, we waited, and finally the door opened a crack, and then we saw an elderly looking woman, in a frayed old cotton overall, and with a dirty apron. Her hair hung down, over her face, as if comb and brush had long not done their work. Her eyes were vacant and expressionless, while her cheeks and nose were lined with red veins. My suspicion that she was a victim of alcohol was confirmed with her first confused and slurred words:

"Hold on a minute, can't you leave me the door in one piece, who are you looking for, what do you want here?" Holmes struggled to conceal his disgust. I tried to get further, by asking if this were where Peter Shephard lived. She looked at me suspiciously, and then muttered, "If you want Peter, you've come too late."

She broke out at once in vulgar and uninhibited laughter, which only stopped, abruptly, when she saw a sovereign in Holmes' hand. She stared greedily at the coin, and stuttered "Peter, Peter is dead..." Holmes quickly spoke to her. "I know. This is yours, if you will please let me see Mr. Shephard's room." She looked again hungrily at the sovereign, and stretched out a dirty finger. Holmes let it fall into her hand, and she stepped back and opened the door wider. Still swaying and struggling to speak clearly, she said, "Come in, then, gentlemen, come and see."

She led us upstairs, to a room on the second floor. We went through a stairway which gave no better impression than the woman herself. At the door of the room she fished under her apron, missed her objective more than once, but then produced a heavy key with which she finally found the keyhole, and opened the door. Now, however, it was our turn to be surprised. I had been ready for anything, given the state of the house and its objectionable owner. But no, the room which we now entered made a clean and ordered impression. The room was even friendly and inviting, although the furnishings were cheap and simple. As I took in all these impressions, Holmes had already begun to search the cupboard, chest of drawers, and bedside. The woman followed him closely, shaking her head and muttering, "If you're looking for money, there's none to be found here, I know, I've tried. And the police were here, and they found nothing."

Holmes looked at her in disgust, but she seemed not to notice. He paced around the room, with rapid steps, his eyes hunting everywhere. "For goodness' sake, Watson, am I wasting our time? I have found nothing here of use…But wait, perhaps this will tell us something." He said no more, but went quickly back to the chest of drawers, on which stood a framed photograph. He took it in both hands, and studied it intently. Then he looked directly at the drunken woman and asked abruptly, "Do you know if Mr. Shephard had any relatives?"

"No, sir, he was as much a loner as I am. Told him often, that mustn't remain so, but he wasn't interested." Another vulgar grunt followed, and then she muttered, "I've always said, you can take a horse to water, but you can't make it drink."

"Then I think I may take this picture with me. If any relatives ask, and would like to have it, you may come to me and ask. Here is my card." With these words he left his visiting card on the chest of drawers, and turned to leave the room. The old woman was, however, suddenly sharp; with a quickness which surprised me, she stood in his way and blocked the doorway. This was followed by a display of apparent innocence, "But sir, I 'm not sure my conscience will allow me to let you simply to take things away… "

I saw how Holmes' eyes narrow, and his lips were pressed thinly together. He held the picture with one hand, and I saw how his other hand was clenched around the head of his stick, so that his knuckles were white. I thought it advisable to move quickly between the two of them, and found a sovereign which I held under the woman's dirty nose. She stopped, and looked again hungrily at the coin. I said quickly, "I think this might reassure your conscience." She nodded and her tongue passed over the cracked lips. Then she grabbed at the coin, and stepped aside, leaving the way free.

As we were about to descend the stairway, she called after us mischievously, "But the gentlemen mustn't be in such a haste. For a sovereign you might have enjoyed more," and she lifted her skirt and torn petticoat. We caught a revolting glimpse of worn-out shoes and grubby, fraying underwear. She broke out again in a wave of vulgar laughter, while we, thoroughly disgusted, withdrew rapidly to the street outside.

Outside the house, our cab was still waiting. Holmes gave our address, 221B Baker Street, and the driver whipped up his horse to a vigorous trot. It was clearly in his mind to leave this disreputable quarter as quickly as he could.

During the first few minutes, we were both silent, after such a disagreeable experience, but then my curiosity left me in peace no longer, and I asked Holmes, what this had to mean.

"Now, Watson, as you surely noticed, Mr. Shephard's room was a model of tidiness. I have seldom seen such a well-made-up bed. The laundry in the chest was also accurately laid together. This tells me clearly, that he was formed by his time in military service. I think Lord Armstrong's assessment of his character was completely justified."

"Holmes, in that you are surely correct. All the same, that does not tell me why you brought with you the photograph. Is there in this picture something particularly striking? I see two men in uniform, both about the same age, around 30 years. One of the two is surely Peter Shephard, and since, as Lord Armstrong said, he had worked for some 15 years in the museum, the picture must have been made nearly twenty years ago. That is certainly interesting, but how on earth does it help us to explain Peter Shephard's death?"

"Ah, Watson, let me explain then that it is not the picture which interested me, but the fact that it was crooked in its frame." I looked at Holmes without grasping his meaning.
.
"Watson, you are surely right in your estimation that the photograph is almost twenty years old. That is however not reflected in its condition. He must have treated it very carefully. It clearly meant much to him, or he would not have framed it and kept it where he could always see it. Would an old soldier with an almost Prussian sense of order have been so careless as to allow such an important picture to be so negligently framed?"

"Ah, surely not."

"You see then, Watson, why the picture aroused my interest. I think that Mr. Shephard has recently opened the frame, and then closed it again in some haste, so that the picture was not properly aligned."

With these words he turned the photograph over. There was a catch on the back which he opened. As he opened the back, their came to light a folded sheet of paper. Although the light was failing, it was enough for us to read the short hand-written message which appeared.

I confirm herewith, that today Peter Shephard, lately in Her Majesty's Military Service, now Watchman in the British Museum, has loaned me the sum of fifty pounds sterling.

London, July 31, 1890   *Brian Hammond*

"A promissory note, a pledge!" I cried out. It seemed that this was something with which not even Holmes had reckoned. I had to go on.

"Oh dear, Holmes, instead of finding something which exonerates Brian Hammond, we seem now to have found something which will bring him to the gallows. Up to now the police have had no motive for a murder, even if two watchmen have heard an argument. That would scarcely have sufficed before a jury. But this pledge could, in the most literal sense, be enough to break his neck."

While I spoke, Holmes had taken the paper and carefully laid it inside his pocketbook. He then closed the frame and secured the catch. Only now did he look at me and say, in complete calm, "Nothing is more deceptive than the apparently obvious".

Then he remained silent, until we reached Baker Street.

A decision

On entering the familiar room at 221B Baker Street for the second time this day, I saw my doctor's bag which I had left here, as Holmes made his impetuous departure. It reminded me that we had been out a long time, and that I had to get back to Mary who would be waiting for me in Kensington. There was immediately within me a battle of loyalties. I must get back into the arms of my dear Mary, and then enjoy an agreeable weekend with her. Equally, however, I felt the urge to continue with Holmes to address our problem, and share in his deliberations. Aware that I could not do both, I was uneasy in my heart. It was then that I heard Holmes' clear voice.

"Dear Watson, please do not concern yourself over the case before us. At the moment I have only fragments and loose ends in my hand. It would be both foolish and dangerous at this stage to attempt to draw conclusions. In such situations one is, in regarding the case, no longer objective, but falls back involuntarily into collecting those indications which only confirm one's preconceived ideas. This tendency, which I have often observed at Scotland Yard, I intend to avoid. You may therefore return reassured to your good wife."

Astonished, I looked at my friend. Once more he had read my thoughts as if they were an open book. I was about to remark on this when he again spoke.

"I am most grateful for your company, my old friend. It was almost like the old days, when you always went with me and were my faithful scribe. Even so, it is time for you to be going, for soon you will have difficulty in finding a free cab, to bring you home. Please present my compliments to your wife."

As he was speaking, Homes had settled himself again, in the posture of a tailor, and reached out for his violin. I might again have said something, but he had already begun, from this instrument, to produce dreadful and unmusical sounds. A casual observer might have thought that he really could not play a violin, and yet I knew, from our long friendship, that he could play it quite beautifully. These painful sounds only rang out when he was struggling to come to terms with a problem standing in his way. When that was so, he had no further awareness of anything else. I picked up my bag, went to the door and looked back to take leave of him.

"Good evening, Holmes," I said quietly, well aware that he would probably not hear me

On my return to Kensington, I was warmly greeted by Mary, and she asked about my day. I told her of my visit to Holmes, and of Professor Hammond, who had made a most favourable impression on me. I next told her of his nephew, suspected of murder. I described to her my fear, that barring a miracle, he was likely to be convicted and hanged.

Mary's generous heart ensured that she felt a spontaneous sympathy for these people. So it was that she at once gave me an energetic reaction, that if anyone could find the way to a miracle, it would be Sherlock Holmes.

"I hope, my dear, that you will prove to be right," I replied.

She looked at me, sensing my unease, and I explained to her the experience we had had at 47 Cudworth Street. I was naturally careful to omit the quite improper offer we had received from the landlady. That is, of course, nothing for a lady's ears. Mary understood however at once that with the discovery of the loan pledge, we would deliver a motive to the prosecution. She was shocked and said,

"But that looks very bad for the young man. What does Holmes think about it?"

Somewhat aggrieved that I had not been able to accompany him in his thoughts, I said, "He is simply sitting in Baker Street and tormenting himself, his violin and Mrs. Hudson."

I looked again at Mary, and it was clear that something was greatly occupying her. Suddenly I realised that she had made a decision; her eyes lit up, and a smile spread over her lips.

"John, my dear, would you be angry with me, if I were to turn you out for the weekend?"

"I beg your pardon, Mary, what do you mean?"

"Well, John, I know how much you dislike it, when the house has to be thoroughly cleaned in your presence. Our maid has kept things in good order, but after our long absence in Robertsbridge, it really is time that the house and the practice are cleaned throughout and made properly fresh. I wanted to have this done over this coming weekend, and it occurs to me that you might well prefer to spend a night in Baker Street. Holmes would surely enjoy your company."

I smiled at her. Her intention thus to relieve me of the hard decision, between our precious time together, and joining Holmes in his newest case, was really very touching. Her questioning, and yet affectionate, expression, as she looked at me, softened again as I stood up, took her hand and drew her to me. I looked at her, deep in her eyes, and said, with all the warmth in my heart,

"Thank you."

A satisfied smile in her face, she stood up to join me to go upstairs to our bedroom.

Returning to Baker Street

After breakfast I packed again my small travelling bag. This, thanks to my army years, took little time. At first I thought to leave my Army revolver at home, but then I thought better of it. As I took my leave of Mary, she urged me to be careful. I had to reassure her repeatedly that I would do so, and finally I made my way again to Baker Street.

When I arrived, I was welcomed by Mrs. Hudson, who told me that Holmes had eaten neither in the evening, nor at breakfast time, that is, since the previous day. He had, however, played his violin painfully, the whole night through. I found a few well-chosen words of sympathy for Mrs. Hudson, and then went to the stair, climbed to the next floor and knocked on Holmes' door. There was no response, and I carefully turned the knob and opened the door. I then stepped into the so familiar room. I was at once enveloped in a dense cloud of smoke, so thick that one might have feared there were a fire, so impenetrable as it was. In fact, it was the product of the many pipes which Holmes had smoked, through the night as he paused from tormenting his violin. I enjoy a good pipe myself, but this was truly insufferable. My eyes filled with tears, and my lungs were burning. I searched for air, and I let my bag fall, stretching out my arms, hoping safely to reach the opposite wall, and a window. Finding one, I released the catch and threw it open.

Breathing deeply in the morning air, I stood a while to recover. When I drew back, the smoke was less. The furnishings were now visible, and I saw that Holmes was in his armchair, sitting cross-legged as he often did, His grey dressing gown hung down over a long nightshirt, and he appeared to be sleeping. His head was sunken to his chest, and his breathing seemed calm and steady. I approached him, and laid a hand on his shoulder. He lifted his head, but the eyes remained closed. He muttered grumpily.

"Mrs. Hudson, I told you I wanted no breakfast. Have I not often enough explained, that I cannot burden my constitution with digestion, when I am working on a new case?"

"My dear friend, you have often tried to convince me of that, but as your doctor and friend, I cannot endorse this plundering of your bodily strength." Holmes opened his eyes and stared.

"Yes, Holmes, you have seen correctly, I am here with you again. Mary has, so to speak, turned me out. I am here in the hope that I might take quarters here until tomorrow evening if that does not disturb you."

By now Holmes had stood up, but still he looked at me with some irritation. Now he was asking me what this meant, so I answered his question.

"My dear Holmes, you can rest reassured. My remark, that Mary has turned me out, was only my way of speaking. She is having the household thoroughly cleaned, and suggested that it might be better if I could spend the time with you."

A smile played on his lips as he listened to me.

"Watson, I have said it before, but such an agreeable thought bears repeating, in your choice of a wife you have had a very successful hand. But now, if you will excuse me, I would like to make myself presentable. Have you breakfasted? Ah, yes, of course. Let us then invite Mrs Hudson to prepare for us a little lunch."

I took my bag into my old room, and then visited Mrs Hudson to express Holmes' wish. She, the good lady, made no complaint over Holmes' irregular habits, being more concerned that he was now indeed ready to eat something. I often thought that she had in my friend not an easy tenant, but I knew that she would have been in no way ready to disappoint him.

Back in our sitting room, I occupied myself for a few moments with 'The Times'. On the inside pages of news reports I found the following item.

Murder in the British Museum

There occurred on the night of Thursday to Friday a murder in the storerooms of the British Museum. The victim was identified as a museum watchman, Peter Shephard, aged 59. It appears that he was stabbed to death during his duty rounds in the Museum. Suspicion falls upon Brian Hammond, aged 22, who has been arrested. Hammond is also an employee of the Museum, an assistant to Dr. Miller, whose accidental death shortly beforehand in the Port of London was already reported. The crime was discovered by two watchmen of the

Museum, who found Mr Hammond at the scene, still holding the murder weapon.

As I read this, the enthusiasm with which I had begun the day seemed to evaporate. Up to now I had tended, despite the discovery of the pledge, to expect that Brian Hammond was not guilty, and that it was our proper task to demonstrate this. Could it, however, in fact be, that he really was guilty? In that case our duty was to demonstrate this. Holmes had indeed made this clear in our conversation with Professor Hammond, but I had tended to erase this possibility from my awareness. Before I let myself become depressed by thought of this option, I resolved to read further in "The Times." In the column of readers' letters, I found the following:

The Mummy's revenge

Sir, it seems to me very clear, that since the moment when the long-awaited Egyptian Mummy reached British soil, those responsible for the transport of the contents of the Egyptian Tomb have been held to account. First, we learned of the death of Dr. Miller, leader of the excavations on site, in an accident by the unloading of the crated goods. Now we learn that his assistant, who was with him in Egypt, has apparently been arrested for murder. And where was this crime committed? In the cellars of the British Museum, just where the Egyptian treasures were stored. Can this be coincidence? No, Sir, it surely cannot! Supernatural powers are here at work. The Mummy, taken from its grave, has been disturbed, and is punishing those responsible. The best course is now to bring those remains by the first possible ship back to Egypt. Who knows, who might next be the victim of its revenge.

Yours, etc., Nigel MacPherson, Esher

Annoyed by this nonsense, I threw the newspaper to the floor.

"Ah, Watson, I suspect that you have seen the reader's letter about the Mummy's revenge."

I had not noticed that Holmes had returned to the room.

"Really, Holmes, I do not know what troubles me most, this reader's letter with its complete nonsense, or the apparently hopeless situation in which Brian Hammond now lies."

"Well, now Watson, at least in respect of Brian Hammond, it seems that all may not yet be lost."

I looked at Holmes in amazement,

"During my observations yesterday in the British Museum, I discovered, on one of the newly painted window frames, part of a shoe print. There were also scratches such as I would expect when an attempt was made, apparently with success, to open the bolt of a window from outside, with a knife. Someone had obviously entered the Museum by this means in the last few days."

"Then that is why you asked Lord Armstrong whether there had recently been an attempt to break into the Museum? But,

43

Holmes, even if that were the case, we cannot automatically deduce that this unknown person killed the watchman. We do not even know whether it all happened on Thursday evening."

"Yes, Watson, we can. As I looked at the packing cases in the cellar, I saw that there were fragments of white paint and scratches, which corresponded to those at the window. Someone had clearly attempted to lift the lid of one of these cases. The knife that he was using was, however, not sufficient to permit this. He was still occupied with this when Peter Shephard, the watchman, surprised him. He stabbed the watchman and fled, in such haste that he left the knife behind."

"Was he afraid of detection, or did he flee on realising what he had done?"

"Either is possible and deserves consideration. I think personally that the sudden appearance of Brian Hammond on the scene was the reason."

"And why was Hammond there at that time?"

"That, Watson, is what we must first clarify. We will therefore, as our next step, visit Hammond's rooms to see what more we can learn about that young man."

"Would it not be better to ask him directly?"

"Normally I would agree with you; we would do that. Since, however, he refuses to explain to his uncle, and to his lawyer, what he was doing in the Museum at night, he is scarcely going to make an exception for us. No, to visit him at this stage of our enquiries is of no value."

At this moment Mrs. Hudson came in with a plate of cold beef sandwiches and a pot of tea. Holmes seemed very hungry, for he took a generous serving. I took simply a cup of tea. Holmes asked me why I had no appetite. I had to explain.

"Holmes, this case seems to be troubling me more than I can describe. It seemed clear; and now there are so many aspects that all we are doing is finding new questions."

"Indeed, Watson, it is often so; the more such a crime seems to be clear and obvious, the more difficult it is, to understand what is really behind it. But do not be troubled, Watson, in this tangle we will surely find the thread which brings us to a clear explanation".

Still more questions

There was still in our minds the impression left by our visit to 47 Cudworth Street, so we were pleased to learn that Bryan Hammond's rooms in Barclay Street were in a better part of London. His landlady, Mrs. Patterson, was an older, obviously conscientious, and almost motherly woman, full of praise for her tenant, Mr. Hammond, whom she described as a friendly, helpful and reliable young man. She was personally convinced that the allegations against him were unfounded, and that there was surely a misunderstanding.

When we explained that our objective was indeed to demonstrate his innocence, she was eager to help. She took us to his rooms. These consisted of a sitting room and bedroom. The rooms were light and friendly, and seemed, for a young man alone, to be surprisingly orderly. Holmes spoke about this to Mrs. Patterson, who admitted that she did help to keep things tidy.

"You see, gentlemen, he spends so much of his time at the Museum. Up to three months ago, he was often there on weekends too."

"Even at the weekends?" I asked.

"Yes, sir, it surprised me too, and I asked him about it. He answered me, that it was not that he was working there, but that he took his pleasure in spending his time in the Library".

I had to say that I found this quite praiseworthy; but now Holmes had a question for Mrs. Patterson. "You said that this was up to three months ago? Do you know why he changed his habits? "

"No, sir, I can't be certain, but I had a suspicion that he had met a young lady and saw her on the weekend."

"What makes you think that, Mrs. Patterson?"

"It was when he asked me if I knew of an address where he might hire an inexpensive suit for evening wear. The prices he had been given were all outside his means, and then I suggested that he might borrow the Sunday suit of my late husband. Admittedly, the cut was not really modern, and the suit had signs of wear, but with a little careful attention it was quite a good fit. And I must say that Mr Hammond looked very presentable."

While Mrs Patterson described this, and while Holmes naturally endorsed her description of Mr. Hammond's gratitude, he had been taking the opportunity to look at the room. He was particularly interested in the writing desk which the young man had been using. He seemed however to have found there nothing of particular interest, despite a close examination, and was about to turn away, when he stopped abruptly. He spoke again to the landlady.

"Mrs. Patterson, while Mr Hammond was in Egypt, you surely emptied the waste paper basket."

"Most certainly, Mr. Holmes! Naturally I did. Indeed, I cleaned everywhere right through, before he returned to London, so that when he came back from those foreign parts, he would feel at home again".

Holmes nodded, and took the waste paper basket in his hand. He emptied the contents onto the writing desk. We all leaned forward to see what he was doing. There were some twenty tickets and programmes for a music hall production at the Elephant and Castle Theatre. There was also a picture frame, of which the glass was broken.

"Mrs. Patterson, would you know who this young woman might be?" asked Holmes, and showed her the picture in the broken frame, which was of a most attractive, dark-haired person.

"I'm sorry, sir, but I never saw her."

"No, Mrs. Patterson, I am not surprised. But I am most grateful for your invaluable help. May we now wish you a good afternoon?"

As Holmes said this, he carefully removed the picture from the broken frame, and took also one of the programmes. He then turned on his heel and sought the door. I took leave of Mrs. Patterson as courteously and as hastily as possible, and hurried after him. He had already summoned a Hansom cab, and was climbing in. I heard him give the address to the driver, namely, the Elephant and Castle Theatre. This would mean quite a long journey across London, so I resolved to ask Holmes the questions which came to mind.

"Tell me, Holmes, did you then find anything in Hammond's rooms, and in the waste paper basket, which might be of importance in the case?"

"Not directly."

"Oh, what do you mean?"

"Well, Watson, as we saw, the rooms only confirm the opinion of Professor Hammond and of his landlady. He is clearly a diligent and ambitious young man, and he has no vices, something which is not self-evident, when we think of Professor Hammond's description of his father. In this respect he seems more to take after his uncle. I fear however that he has fallen a victim of a relationship with a woman with whom he was infatuated, but which was bound to end in disappointment. Through this, I fear, he may have fallen from that straight and narrow way which we would expect of him."

"I'm sorry, Holmes, but despite my best intentions, I have not quite followed you. It is clear to me that he may have fallen for the woman in the picture, three months ago. That this had a rude end seems very probable, for why would a young man otherwise throw away the picture he treasured? But why do you conclude that the affair had no future, and must fail? And how did Brian Hammond in your view fall from the straight and narrow, as you put it?"

"It is really a rather trivial conclusion, to which I came courtesy of the theatre tickets and the programme cards. The oldest were from April, when Brian's infatuation began. From that time on, he regularly attended the Saturday and Sunday performances, until going to Egypt. My dear Watson, I have little experience of such things, but I scarcely believe that a man wishing to impress a young woman will attend week for week always the same performances on Saturdays and Sundays. I conclude that he did not go to attend the performances, but went there to meet her because she was one of the performers. Our solid, reliable and perhaps conservative Mr Hammond would certainly be a very different personality compared with someone who was accustomed to appearing on the stage, particularly on the stage of a theatre such as this, in southeast London. No, this was an infatuation which must come to an unhappy end."

I had to interrupt Holmes' discourse, as I was still not quite assured.

"But Holmes, how do you come to believe she is a performer? Could it not be that she works at the theatre, perhaps as cloakroom attendant?"

Holmes seemed at first irritated. Then he smiled, an amused smile. "My dear friend, if the woman is not a performer, why would he need an evening suit? Why would he always attend the same performances? Why would he have hoarded his tickets and programmes? And now, if that is not enough to convince you, look again at the picture, and tell me if she looks like a cloakroom attendant."

I had to admit that Holmes was right; but before I could follow him with any further remark, he picked up his interrupted discourse.

"Again, starting with the theatre tickets and our observation that the object of this infatuation is an artistic performer, we can deduce that he had already left the straight and narrow way. We learned from his landlady that his pocketbook does not permit him any excesses. Yet he found the money for two theatre tickets each week. That alone comes to a respectable sum. Moreover, he has certainly, in his efforts to impress this lady, bought her presents. Where could he have found the money? He has no close friends who might have made him a loan. And here he works in a museum which has so many exhibits, many of which it cannot use, that it will not be noticed if something were taken and sold outside."

I was again astonished by this clear statement. I had to find words of my own for that which Holmes had rather more elegantly described.

"You mean that Brian Hammond had stolen from the British Museum?"

"Quite so, Watson, and this will surely be the reason why he wants to tell neither his uncle, nor his lawyer, what brought him to be in the museum at night."

"Holmes, that all now seems very clear. But there is also the question of the promissory note, the pledge. As you yourself said, he seems to have no-one who would lend him money. It appears, however, that Peter Shephard was ready to do so".

"Yes, as you say, Watson, and in that matter I am still without an answer. But have you any further questions?"

"I have indeed, Holmes. Up to now it has been your concern to prove the innocence of Brian Hammond. What you have told me has brought another, unknown, person, into our considerations, who obviously broke into the museum, and killed the night watchman who discovered him. Is it not equally necessary to search for this person?"

"Watson, if I could do that, you may believe that I would have done so long ago. This person has behaved so unusually that ever since I have been aware of his existence, he has occupied me. At the moment there seems to be no other way forward, though, than to study as carefully as possible the behaviour of Mr. Hammond. We must not forget that that is what Professor Hammond has charged us to do."

I nodded my understanding, but now there was another question.

"But, Holmes, you also spoke of the unusual behaviour of the unknown person. Do you refer to the murder of the watchman?"

"Yes, that too, Watson. In the first place, however, it is the nature of the break-in which occupies me. Just consider, Watson. Our thief is certainly not a beginner, for he succeeded in entering without leaving any more traces than I myself discovered. He entered in the entrance hall of the museum, which leads to exhibition rooms containing some of the richest treasures and precious stones. Our practiced thief could have helped himself and easily made his escape with his findings. But what does he do? He descends to the cellar and attempts to open the crates that are stored there. I would ask you to consider why that was so."

I looked vaguely at Holmes and had to shrug my shoulders. Holmes gave me the answer.

"Because he was commissioned to steal something, which others wanted. He did not however know in which of the packing cases he would find it, He tried with several."

"Then Holmes, we must ask ourselves what he was looking for. What might it be?"

"Of that I have no idea, Watson. But it was important enough for him to kill for it. It was otherwise not necessary to kill Shephard. Just think, the watchman was an elderly war invalid with a stiff leg. He represented no danger to a thief who only wanted to get away unrecognised."

Holmes still had me puzzled. I had to ask him, "What then could have incited the thief to kill the watchman?"

Holmes was thinking again, and answered, almost talking to himself, "He wanted to conceal that someone was interested in the content of the crates."

At the Elephant & Castle Theatre

It was already late afternoon when we arrived at the theatre. The programme which we had brought showed that the evening performance did not start until 8 o'clock.

My fear that we might have undertaken this long journey in vain was dispelled by the theatre director, who, when he met us, told us that Saturday afternoon was always the time of the dress rehearsal. When Holmes showed him the photograph which we had found in Brian Hammond's room, he at once said, "Oh, yes, that is Miss Loretta. We all consider her to be really beautiful. She performs with our Italian magician." He looked at his watch, and then said, "They must be almost ready to rehearse; if we hurry, you should be in time to see their number as they perform it, on stage."

As we went into the theatre, we saw that the stage where the performance would take place was closed off by the main curtain. We sat down just as a man in evening dress stepped out from behind the curtain, onto the illuminated stage, and announced the coming number.

"Ladies and gentlemen, we now have for your incredulous delight and entertainment the one and only, the Great Rodolfo and his enchanting, irresistible assistant, Signorina Loretta!"

The curtain rose, and we saw a pair of figures of vaguely southern European appearance, who bowed as if to the audience. The Great Rodolfo wore a tail coat, a wide cape and a top hat. With his rather exaggerated gestures, he looked more greasy than elegant. For Miss Loretta, I can only say that her costume was extremely suggestive and so provocative that it is difficult to describe it in written words. Her sleeveless bodice seemed only to consist of a corset with a most revealing neckline. There was a skirt, but this, while it reached behind her to the floor, was so short in front that it barely reached her knee. It must be said that she was a most dramatic, breath-taking beauty, and to my shame I must admit that once their performance started, and apart from some endearing rabbits and doves, I remembered little of the tricks which were performed by the Great Rodolfo. Miss Loretta had commanded my full attention

After the performance, we went again to meet the theatre director who took us to the dressing rooms of the magician and his assistant. We waited then to meet the performers. I was absorbed by a variety of mostly glittering costumes, but Holmes immediately occupied himself with the artists' make-up which he found on the dressing tables. When the two artists arrived, he turned, meeting them with a warm smile and said enthusiastically,

"Oh, Signor Rodolfo, e la Signorina Loretta, che e stato uno spettacolo patetico. Lei, Signor Rodolfo, sei un asino. E lei, la Signorina Loretta e une mucco".

I was shocked to hear him, as even if my knowledge of Italian was poor compared to his, it was enough for me to recognise that he had just described the performance as miserable, and to describe the two performers respectively as a donkey and a cow. I expected some sort of indignant reaction, at least from the beautiful Loretta, but all that happened was that she looked uncertainly at Holmes, smiled and looked for reassurance from the Great Rodolfo. It would not have surprised me if his reaction had been violent, but no, he grinned broadly under his generous moustache, seized the hand of Holmes and shook it warmly. As he stopped, he said in broken English,

"Thank you for your compliment. But we can continue in English, as we are guests in this wonderful country."

"As you wish, then, Signor Rodolfo," replied Holmes in a severe voice, "But then you may prefer to give up this absurd cheap Italian imitation, and tell me your proper name."

The Great Rodolfo looked sharply at my friend, but Holmes continued unperturbed.

"This whole Italian show is nothing but a deception. It is the walnut oil on your dressing table which gives you a dark complexion, and even then you must be more careful in applying it. In your wrinkles it has left a darker stain. And with 'Dr. Tempelton's Hair Colouring,' which is also on your table, you have both achieved a dense head of black hair. Even so, you should use it more often, as at the roots your own red hair is already clearly visible. Finally, in securing your artificial moustache, you really should use another adhesive. That which you have causes an all too obvious red irritation of the skin".

The Great Rodolfo attempted at first to contradict Holmes, but then fell silent. His smiling face had changed; he was now ugly and defensive.

"All right then, tell me what you want from us," he demanded.

Holmes, completely self-possessed, replied, "Now, as I said before, what is your real name, and from where do you come?"

"My name is Joseph McGinty and this is my wife Molly. We both come from Glasgow."

"There", said Holmes, "that already sounds better. And now a question for you, Mrs. McGinty. Do you know a young man named Brian Hammond?"

Before answering, she looked searchingly at her husband. He nodded, and she turned back to answer Holmes. "Yes, I do know Brian Hammond. He was one of my admirers. For at least three months he came regularly, except when he went to Egypt, and saw each performance every weekend. He also took me out and sometimes made me presents of jewellery."

As she said this, I saw Miss Loretta, or Molly McGinty, talking of this with an almost shocking and self-evident clarity in front of her husband. I looked from the one to the other. How could McGinty simply accept that his wife would go out with other men, and accept presents from them? He must have suspected my thoughts, because he suddenly spoke up.

"If you find our behaviour unusual, remember that we are illusionists. We not only sell the audience a show with illusions, but we also address the men who cannot take their eyes off Molly. For a few weeks they can live in their illusion that Molly might go with them. The presents which she receives are for us a valuable resource for the times without engagements."

I was still shocked, but Holmes had his next question ready for Molly McGinty.

"When did you tell Brian Hammond the truth?"

"That was this last Tuesday evening. He came again, unexpectedly, to the theatre, and waited at my dressing room with a beautiful bouquet of roses, and then he knelt before me to propose marriage. I could do no more than to tell him that I was already married. I almost felt sorry for the poor lad. He was at first completely confused, and then furious, and finally he turned and rushed out, apparently almost in panic."

As I listened, I saw McGinty turn back to Holmes, and demand,

"All right, then, what is it that you really want from us?"

"That was all, thank you. You are of no further interest to me," said Holmes coldly. He turned on his heel, and was about to leave. However, McGinty was not satisfied. He blocked the way, and asked aggressively,

"What's all this about? Are you after something from us? Do you want to be a partner? It's not a bad deal if we could work together."

I saw how Holmes' features, up to now carefully controlled, suddenly filled with distaste. Before McGinty had realised what was happening, he was on the floor, the victim of one of those Baritsu holds which had so often helped Holmes out of difficult situations. Still disgusted, he stepped over McGinty, and left the dressing room. I could only do the same and be pleased that we could leave the theatre without any further difficulty.

At the Rat & Raven

It was early in the evening when we left the theatre, and it was already difficult, in southeast London, to find a free cab. Once that had been achieved, Holmes gave the driver his destination, an address in Wapping, Old Gravel Lane, near the Eastern Dock. This long journey would lead us again into East London, but this time north of the Thames. The address seemed vaguely familiar to me, but it was no use asking Holmes, as he was already deeply immersed in his thoughts. I leaned back, closed my eyes and tried to remember. Suddenly it came back to me – the Rat and Raven public house, which was kept by Holmes' old acquaintance Porky. His real name was Shinwell Johnson, and he had run up against the law with various minor criminal activities. Holmes had brought him to conviction, and he had served his time.

He had then succeeded in making a new start, something for which he had to thank Sherlock Holmes who recommended him further, because as a person with previous convictions he would scarcely have been able to obtain a licence as innkeeper. Porky never forgot it; and showed his gratitude on many occasions when he was able, discreetly of course, to pass on useful tips on events in the London, and especially docklands', underworld. Indeed, through the customers who frequented his pub, he still maintained some old contacts in that world from which he had now freed himself.

We had last seen him in connection with the case of the Thames murders, where, without knowing the background, he was nevertheless able to help us with invaluable information. I was now wondering if he would again be able to help us. Even so, it was a situation requiring great care and discretion, for he dared not risk being thought to betray those around him. Holmes always took the greatest care to avoid compromising him.

Our cab turned into Old Gravel Lane. Holmes knocked with his stick on the roof, the signal to the driver above that he should stop. So it was that as we alighted, I was surprised to see that we were at the far end of the street from Porky's public house. I took a little longer to descend to the pavement, and Holmes had already paid the fare. Clearly something more was given, for the driver was most grateful. Then, however, he turned his cab and made his way out of Wapping as fast as he could, something for which I could hardly reproach him. Before I could ask Holmes what we were about to do, he answered, as so often, the question for me.

"You will surely ask yourself why we have chosen to take a stroll, on this cool evening, and in this uninviting district. Allow me to explain."

He set off briskly and I followed as best I could. Old Gravel Lane was a narrow street, crudely laid with cobblestones, and practically in darkness. There was an unmistakeable smell of fish in the air, for the Shadwell Market, which was known for suppling fish both to the poor and working people of the East End, and to the house servants of the better society in their houses near the City, was quite near. But nobody stayed longer than they must, for the district was very disreputable, and, as we must fear, probably dangerous. We were now far from Baker Street, and not only as measured by the distance. Although the street seemed deserted, I was aware that Holmes was always vigilant, as he walked along.

"Now, Watson, let me explain. I am concerned for Porky's safety. That is why we are walking here. You know what sort of clients he has to serve. In his public bar we would be very conspicuous. Some of his customers might be curious about us. Any suggestion that he might be telling us things better kept quiet, and Porky's health, indeed his life, might be in danger."

I followed perfectly, and commented only that it would be foolish to provoke trouble. But why, then, were we here, if not to see Porky?

"We will see Porky, but we will not meet him in the public bar. We will be in the cellar."

So it was, that we walked past the Rat and Raven, turned left into an even narrower street, and walked towards Red Lion Street. We stopped, however, where the cellar entrance to the Rat and Raven, at the side of the house, lay in the pavement. This was where supplies of coal, beer barrels and more were unloaded from delivery carts. Holmes lifted the catch and was evidently satisfied to find it unlocked. He opened the catch, and lifted the heavy cellar door, and found a dark lantern on the top step of the stairs down to the cellar. Then he smiled and muttered,

"Porky got my message."

I must admit that I knew nothing of these arrangements.

Descending a few steps, we could lower the cellar door over our heads, and went further, with the lantern. There was a large room, in which the lantern gave a warm light. It was untidy and damp, which did not surprise me, and everywhere were crates and barrels. In an open space stood a large barrel, and there were three wooden boxes arranged around it. On the barrel was a large oil lamp. Holmes lit it and the cellar reflected the yellow light. At this moment we heard steps on the wooden stair from the public rooms, and then we saw Porky. He came to us, put down his lantern, and shook our hands warmly. With a broad smile he said,

"Oh, Mr. Holmes, Dr. Watson! It's good to have you here again, in my humble house! I must admit that it's the first time I've had guests down here. But that's how you wanted it, Mr. Holmes. Now, what will it be?"

"Well, now, Porky, how about a good dinner? I think that would be best. And you, Watson? "

I could only agree.

"Wonderful, gentlemen, wonderful," said Porky still beaming. Burt then he was thoughtful. "Are you sure you wouldn't rather sit upstairs in the bar-room?"

"No, Porky, we will be very comfortable here. I am right in thinking that the barrel and seats are for us?"

"That's so, sir, but…" Holmes left him no more chance to insist, and so we took our places at this homely supper-table.

"And what can I bring you? I've got a chicken pie, and there is jellied fish with baked potatoes."

Holmes and I decided upon the chicken pie, the more so because Porky rolled his eyes and absent-mindedly stroked his broad apron front as he spoke of it.

"And then you will bring us two tankards of your excellent beer," said Holmes, "and bring one for yourself."

"Thank you, Mr. Holmes, I always say, you can always tell a real gentleman."

Porky's meal was generous and was quite excellent. When our plates and tankards were empty, we found Porky again by us, asking if we needed anything else.

Holmes spoke again. "Well, Porky, first you will fill up our tankards, and your own, and then you will please join us for a while." Porky did as he was requested, muttering that Mr. Holmes was a gentleman to the soles of his boots. He was surely correct.

Within a few minutes we were all three sitting around the barrel, and drinking one another's goods health. Holmes then raised the question, if he had had an opportunity to keep his ear to the ground, as he went about his business.

"Yes, Mr. Holmes, I did put out a few feelers in different directions. On Brian Hammond there was nothing which might be considered questionable. It did however come to my ear that about three months ago, he had brought two antique pictures to a pawnshop."

"Really, Porky? And would you, by chance, know which pawn shop that was?"

"Well, yes, I do," said Porky with some pride. "A Jewish art expert, Joshua Goldstone, has a pawnshop in the City Road. I had quite a long conversation with him about Brian Hammond. I am sure you would like to know what he told me."

Holmes had closed his eyes and held his fingertips pressed together, as he so often did when he was listening intently. A smile lay on his lips as he nodded his approval.

"I have known Mr Goldstone for a long time, he's a fine man, and he told me that the two paintings were historical and very valuable. He would gladly have bought them from Mr. Hammond, but no, his offer was refused, and it was made clear that the pictures were only to be pawned. This was despite the price Mr Goldstone offered, to buy them, being three times more than he could offer as a loan."

Porky stopped and looked at us. I suggested that he should continue.

"Mr. Goldstone told me that the date agreed for redeeming the pawned objects was yesterday, Friday, August 1st. Mr. Hammond came back to the pawnshop on Wednesday afternoon, and Mr. Goldstone thought he would redeem the pictures then. But no, Mr. Hammond begged to be given more time to raise the money. Mr Goldstone is not a hard man, and felt very sorry, for he saw that Hammond was evidently in great distress, on the verge of breakdown, but he had to refer him to the conditions of the loan. It was clear that Hammond had until Friday to repay the loan. When that was not the case, the pictures would pass into the possession of Mr. Goldstone. With that a deeply disturbed Mr Hammond left the pawnshop. Ready to believe he would never see him again, Mr. Goldstone was already considering at what profit he could sell the pictures, in the right circumstances; but on Thursday afternoon, Mr Hammond came back, brought the money and redeemed the pictures.

Porky had finished his account, and he looked expectantly at Holmes. Opening his eyes, Holmes smiled and said,

"Splendid, Porky, quite perfect. I am much obliged to you."

I saw how proud Porky was, to have been of service to us, and he rubbed his hands together to say, "Well, I am only too pleased to be able to help."

We drank again to one another, and then there was a satisfied pause, until Holmes asked,

"And what is the news about the late Dr. Miller? Have you learned anything interesting about him?"

"Very little, really, Mr. Holmes. When he was a young man he liked to bet on the horses, but he seems usually to have chosen the wrong ones. If you ask the bookies, they think he must have lost a lot of money in this way. Three years ago, however, he married, and I was told that he no longer bet on the horses. His wife came of a good family, as she was the only daughter of Sir Charles Winter and she brought with her the villa in Lexington Street. On Tuesday Dr. Miller was the victim of a severe accident which cost him his life. You will know about that. But that was all I learned about Dr. Miller."

He stopped here, but did not seem at ease. He stared down into his beer tankard, holding it with both hands. "Porky, what is it?" Holmes had recognised at once that something was troubling Porky, who began to speak thoughtfully, even hesitantly.

"Mr. Holmes, I don't know how I should describe what it is, but there is something about Dr. Miller which is not clear. My old mate Bill had whispered to me that Dr. Miller had been refused admission to various clubs, barred allegedly because of his gambling debts. Eight weeks ago, all his notes of debt were redeemed, but Bill couldn't say who had paid them. He only knew that it was not Dr. Miller."

"Yes, and what then?" asked Holmes, obviously concerned by this news.

Porky lifted his head and looked furtively over his shoulder, as if he feared an unwelcome listener in the cellar. He leaned forward and began to whisper.

"I asked a few friends if they had heard anything. There was a wall of silence, but it wasn't that they didn't know anything, but because they were afraid. Then I looked up Bill, to see if he knew any more. I hardly recognised him, for he looked as if he had been between two millstones. When I mentioned Dr. Miller, he denied ever mentioning him to me. And as I left, he earnestly begged me not to stick my nose into things that don't concern me."

Porky had finished. We sat silently for a few moments, and then Holmes spoke gently, breaking the tension.

"Porky, I thank you from the heart for the trouble you have taken. I am deeply sorry that our questions have obviously brought you into a threatening situation. I advise you to lie low for a while. You have helped me very much, and I will not see you suffer for it."

Porky looked up and seemed somewhat relieved. Holmes continued,

"And now let us forget all this, and remember fondly something of past times. Let us fill our tankards, and you can then come back to us to tell us some of your old publican's stories!"

Porky relaxed, and responded to this invitation, so that the sound of laughter soon filled the cellar. Porky was a natural story-teller, and his yarns were always good.

Setting out again to return to Baker Street, it was now quite late. If Holmes had seemed relaxed and light-hearted in Porky's cellar, I saw that at heart he had been seriously occupied by what he had heard. Fortunately, as Holmes had instructed our hansom driver of earlier to return at 10 o'clock to fetch us, and had already given him a substantial tip, he had kept word, and so we found him waiting. Even so, when he heard us he raised his whip threateningly, but then saw and recognised us. He lowered the whip, watched us climb in, and with a single gesture he turned the horse and set off back to the City. He lost no time in getting out of the always menacing world of the East end docks, and perhaps rightly so.

Now alone with Holmes, I hoped to learn more of his thoughts, on several of the things we had heard. He however remained silent. There was no change in him as we reached 221B Baker Street. But instead of reviewing the case, Holmes simply wished me goodnight, and disappeared into his room. I could only do the same, hopeful that despite all that was turning in my head, I might indeed find sleep.

Scotland Yard

It was long before I found the sleep I needed, and even then it was uneasy. My dreams were confused and menacing. At one time I found myself in the British Museum with Holmes, just in front of the great glass shrine which Lord Armstrong had shown me. This time it was not empty, but held a real mummy. My head seemed to hear a voice telling us that one should not disturb the rest of the dead. Dr. Miller and Brian Hammond had received the punishment they deserved, and now it was the turn of Holmes and myself. Then as the words died away, the mummy slowly rose up from the waist, and sat up before us. At that moment I awoke with a start, and realised with relief that I was in my bed. I saw that it was already daylight outside, and resolved to get up and at least avoid the risk of more nightmares. I washed and dressed, and entered our room, where I found to my surprise that Holmes was already at the writing desk, reading a telegram.

"Good morning, Watson", he called out, clearly in the best of spirits.

"Good morning, Holmes", I replied, trying to give my voice a degree of unconcerned interest which I did not feel.

"Hello, what is troubling you, Watson? Are you feeling unwell? You certainly look rather pale".

"I fear I slept badly," I replied. Holmes' obviously serious concern encouraged me to tell him of my nightmare, even if it made me feel rather foolish. As I concluded, he looked at me and spoke gently.

"My dear friend, in view of everything you have seen and heard in the last forty-eight hours, it seems to me only normal, that your over-wrought imagination has struggled to come to terms with it all. That must surely also be your experience as a doctor. Moreover, this case has many aspects which may appear strangely mysterious and unnatural. That I can well understand, as I too have been caught out by similar thoughts. Allow me to remind you, as I have said before, that where nothing stimulates our fantasy, we will find nothing to fear. This case has however something about it which is hidden from our sight, troubling and puzzling, which challenges our fantasy."

Holmes' words had their effect; I was already feeling better when Mrs. Hudson appeared with breakfast, which quickly completed my recovery. I almost felt ready for new challenges and surprises, so I asked Holmes about the telegram which he had been reading. Did it contain anything significant for the matter in hand?

"Watson, it is most important. It has delivered a missing piece in our puzzle".

I waited, naturally curious, for his explanation.

"My brother Mycroft has at my request had a search made in the War Ministry, for the records of Archibald Hammond and Peter Shephard, and has confirmed that both belonged to the so-called Wolseley Ring, an elite troop of officers and soldiers. Twenty years ago, on the African Gold Coast, they built up an army to suppress rebellion. Mycroft could tell me that Peter Sheppard had been severely wounded during the siege and capture of the town of Kumesi in January 1874. His left leg was shattered and he would have died, falling into the hands of the rebels, had not Archibald Hammond saved him by carrying him through the enemy lines".

"My goodness, Holmes, that was surely a heroic effort." I had to say it as I thought how, in Afghanistan, I was saved by similar courage which saved my life, just as Archibald Hammond had saved Peter Shephard's life.

"So thought obviously General Wolseley, who proposed that Archibald Hammond, a brave officer, might be granted an honourable early retirement and sent back to Britain. But you will recall the account of Professor Hammond. Archibald refused the offer of repatriation, and chose to stay in Africa. Peter Shephard was sent back, after a first recovery, to Britain as a war invalid. He found things very difficult, even as an officer, but finally found employment, if only as a watchman at the British Museum".

As Holmes concluded, we sat silently for some minutes together. Each of us was absorbed by our own thoughts. However, there came then to Holmes' expression a faintly sardonic smile. Then he spoke to me.

"I fear, Watson, that your readers, should you one day ever write the account of this case for them, will conclude that I was singularly blind to the obvious."

That surprised me greatly, and it was a while before I could ask,

"Good Heavens, Holmes, what gives you that idea?"

"Why, I needed Mycroft, to make clear to me an obvious and self-evident conclusion that Peter Shephard and Archibald Hammond served in the same regiment."

"But my dear friend, how might you have guessed that?" I asked, still somewhat puzzled.

"Not guessed, Watson, but deduced! The evidence lay here in my hands, and indeed in yours too."

"Holmes, you are talking in riddles! What evidence do you mean?"

"The framed photograph in Shephard's room. Do you remember, Watson, how I said that the person portrayed there was of no importance. That was an error, because the one was, as you supposed, Peter Shephard, and the second person was Archibald Hammond."

"But Holmes, how could we even suspect that the second man was Archibald Hammond?"

Holmes did not reply, but went to his desk, picked up the photograph and laid it on the table in front of me. "Now, Watson, recall your meeting with Professor Hammond, and then look at the photograph." He started to recite the dominant features.

"Here are the same characteristics, the broad face, the small eyes wide apart, the same wide nose, the fold in the chin and the distinctive ear lobes…."

Quite amazed, I burst out with, "But Holmes, you are right! Now that you have made it obvious, I have to agree. The man illustrated here looks just how I might have imagined a young Professor Hammond to be."

Holmes spoke ruefully. "You see, Watson, you have seen the obvious, to which I was blind."

"Come, Holmes, you had to push it under my nose for me to see it."

He ignored my observation. I therefore, before he could slip into one of his depressive moods, asked quickly,

"What are you then going to do next?"

He thought carefully for a few moments, and then replied as if from a great distance. "I think it is now time to pay a visit to our taciturn friend, Brian Hammond. Would you like to accompany me, Watson?"

I assured him wholeheartedly that I would on no account miss this moment. It was not long before we were on the way to visit Brian Hammond in his cell.

We were at first surprised, on a Sunday, outside Scotland Yard, to meet Inspector Lestrade, who had obviously just paused in his work to take lunch nearby. I knew however that he often had tasks which made unusual calls on him. He was equally surprised to see us, asking then somewhat light-heartedly, what we found to do here on a Sunday. His small dark eyes took in our every movement, and this sharp study only enhanced his somewhat rat-like features. Holmes told him that we were planning to talk with Brian Hammond, and Lestrade assured us that it was a hopeless project. The young man was quite uncooperative, and would talk with nobody, not even his lawyer or his uncle. Holmes said nothing, but took a page from his notebook and wrote quickly on it. Then he gave it to Inspector Lestrade, saying, "Please give this to Mr Hammond. And then we will see, whether he will talk to me."

Lestrade did not hide his amusement. "I wager a sovereign, that you will be wasting your time. Come, Mr. Holmes, will you take me on?"

Just a shadow of a smile passed over Holmes' face as he nodded his agreement. Lestrade went back inside, convinced of an easy win. Five minutes later, however, he was back again, his head no longer held so high. In his hand he held his own sovereign, which he reluctantly dropped into Holmes' outstretched hand. Without a further word, he left us, to go

75

across the street to the restaurant he had first had in mind when we had met him.

We were then escorted by a policeman to the cell where we could be alone, briefly, with Brian Hammond. Holmes introduced himself, and explained that he was acting on behalf of Brian's uncle, to establish what was the connection between Hammond and the murdered watchman. Hammond crouched on a stool, listening at first silently. At these words, however, he leapt up and cried out,

"I did not kill Peter!"

Holmes spoke gently. "Mr. Hammond, I know that, but the matter cannot so easily be settled. Please sit down again, and tell me about your life in England. I will be especially interested in the events of the last few days, and please omit nothing, even if you think it might be used against you. If you are open and honest with me, I think I can help you."

The young man looked doubtful. He sat again on his stool, and I took a seat on the bench on the opposite wall. I noted what he said. At first his explanations were hesitant and unsure, as he described the time spent living with his uncle, and his story corresponded to that which we had already heard from Professor Hammond. It was clear that he was just as affectionately disposed towards his uncle, as the latter was to him. Of his life in London we learned no more than we already knew from his landlady. Next, however, he spoke of his meeting Miss Loretta, and of falling in love with her. He told us how he wanted to offer her something, but that the means were lacking, so that he gave way to temptation and took for himself the two miniatures from the British Museum store rooms. He did not intend to sell them, but to pawn them and redeem them later. He would thus bring them back, before their loss was noticed. Here Holmes interrupted his narrative to ask how he would have intended to raise the sum needed to redeem them.

"I expected to get the money from Dr. Miller. After I had helped him with the excavations, he had given me a bonus, because my knowledge of Arabic had been so helpful. Then, as we prepared the transfer of the contents of the tomb to the port for shipment, he again promised me a bonus. If that were to be as much as the first time, then I had the money to redeem the miniatures safely in view. I had however secretly hoped that there might be even more to come, because now I was to be alone responsible for the packing and transportation of the excavated objects."

"But surely this was Dr. Miller's task? You were, after all, only his assistant?"

"Quite so, Mr. Holmes, but as we reached Cairo, Dr. Miller, who had been looking very unwell, told me that he was not able to work and would have to stay in the hotel. He was certainly very nervous, and had been much of the time; and I could agree that he now looked much worse.

"Since time was already pressing, for the packing and loading in Egypt, and then up to the date of the exhibition in the museum, he asked me to do all that was necessary. The exhibition material was by now in Cairo, well-packed and guarded, but the preparation of the papers, the release by the Egyptian authorities and the formalities with Customs took a long time, nearly ten days. I hoped all along that he would feel better, and help me, but he insisted he must stay in the hotel." Finally he recovered, and came with me to see the contents of the tomb, ready for the transport to the port for loading on the next ship."

"And then?" asked Holmes.

"Once our cargo was on board, we could rest a little. The voyage itself was no problem. We had good weather, and the *Bokhara* made good time, some 13 knots. In twelve days, on Saturday evening, a week ago, she arrived in the Port of London. Indeed, Dr. Miller would have started unloading at once, but we could not obtain so quickly the approval of the London Customs. That troubled him visibly, and when I asked him about my bonus, he only turned on his heel in irritation and said nothing. I resolved to speak to him again when we had seen the packing cases unloaded. This began on Tuesday, and Dr. Miller was constantly pressing the workpeople to work faster. This was not really his manner, and I think he was already afraid that all would not be ready for the exhibition. Indeed, he should perhaps not have been at the ship's side.

It was just in the middle of this work that the accident occurred. A rope broke, a sling fell apart, and a crate slipped out and fell, and trapped Dr Miller between two other crates. He screamed with pain, and the awful sound still rings in my ears whenever I think of it. And then it took so dreadfully long to release him and get him to the hospital in Whitechapel. It was in any case too late; on arrival at the hospital, he was already dead, a victim of the internal injuries he had suffered.

The shock hit me very hard, and it was only later, as I began to recover, that I realised that there would now be no bonus from Dr. Miller. That meant that I could not redeem the stolen miniatures. In the Museum, someone would notice the loss, and suspicion must fall on me. I would lose my job, and my uncle would surely turn from me, as I was a disappointment to him. I was desperate and found nowhere to turn. I had no other friends, and I was despondent. Then I thought of Loretta. She was the only person who had ever told me that she loved me. I went to ask her to marry me. I felt that with her beside me, I could better bear the shame of being found a thief. When I tried to propose to her, she told me bluntly that she was already married. My world collapsed around me, and I had to admit the bitter reality, that I had been nothing more than an infatuated fool and that my weakness had been exploited.

"On Wednesday I went to the pawnbroker, in the hope that he could give me an extension. He could not. In my desperation, I thought of stealing another object, from the museum, and pawning that, in order to redeem the miniatures. Who knows where such a vicious spiral can end? But Heaven be praised, it did not come to this. I had already picked out a small Roman sculpture, to hide in my pocket. Peter Shephard surprised me, and asked me what was going on. At first I wanted to deny it all, and we argued. Suddenly my nerves were at an end, and I broke down and told him the whole story.

"As I finished, he looked at me quietly, and said simply, that all would be well, and that I must have no more fear. He would lend me the money, and leave me as long as I needed to pay it back. When I asked him why he should do this, he explained that my father had once in the African wars saved his life, and that now he had an opportunity, at least posthumously, to do something in return. You cannot imagine my relief, as I received the money from him, and was able to redeem the miniatures on Thursday. I was ready to bring them back on Thursday night to the museum, and replace them in the store-room.

That was when I found Peter lying on the floor, a great knife still standing up in his body. Without thinking further, I pulled out the knife, and it was just then that two other watchmen found me, with Peter lying dead on the floor and a bloodstained knife in my hand".

He stopped, and Holmes spoke gently to him.

"Thank you, Mr. Hammond. You have described these events clearly and honestly, and confirmed my expectations. I can now demonstrate your innocence of this murder, but at this stage I do not know how we can deal discreetly with the theft of the miniatures."

With these words, Holmes stood up, knocked energetically on the heavy oak door of the cell, and waited for the guard to open it. In the meantime Brian looked first at Holmes and then at me, incredulous. I could however say nothing, and so could only shrug my shoulders and try to smile encouragingly, before leaving the cell with Holmes.

Seeking coherence

As we left Scotland Yard, we had no problem hailing a hansom. Holmes gave the address, Lexington Street, and I knew I had heard this address already. I could not place it, however, nor its connection to our task. There were too many questions turning around in my head, and I hoped that Holmes might answer them. I resolved to ask him directly.

"Holmes, what did you write on the note which you gave Lestrade, which persuaded Brian Hammond to see us?"

Homes was, I realised, a little annoyed, that I should break the silence which he needed. But he answered "Goldstone Miniatures"

"And that was all?" I asked, surprised.
.
"Yes, Watson, Mr. Hammond saw from this that somebody knew about the stolen and pawned miniatures. Whether such a person was intending to use the information for or against him, he could not know. To be clear on that, he had to see me."

I nodded, and he added, "But it had to be non-committal and offer no hint, or Lestrade would have become suspicious".

With this he had surely succeeded. I could imagine how Inspector Lestrade occupied his mind over his luncheon, searching for a meaning in those two words, and why they produced in Hammond such a remarkable change of heart. If this were amusing, however, the next question was critical.

"Holmes, you have never explained to me why the two miniatures can exonerate Hammond."

"Oh, I am sorry. Did I not? While we were in the British Museum cellars, looking at the scene of the murder, I carefully examined the packing cases which were standing there. Do you remember?"

"Yes, Holmes, I do. I also recall that you had described scratches on some of the crates, which told you that attempts had been made with a knife to open some of them. It was this that added to your suspicion that a paid thief was looking for something specific."

"Quite so, Watson, but I not only found those traces. Something else aroused my interest. Bloodstains! The top of the crates was covered in bloodstains."

"Oh, so that was it. But that is surely no surprise, when we knew that the body lay on the cellar floor in a large pool of blood. That tells me that an artery was cut, with the result that blood, under pressure, would be thrown in all directions".

"Yes, Watson, very good; your remark is quite correct" I was naturally pleased that he should say so, but obviously there was more to come, to explain why it was so important.

"You see, Watson, as I said, blood splashes were everywhere, and even on the miniatures which were lying there. Only, the blood was only on the underside."

I must have shown in my expression that I still did not understand, because Holmes looked at me impatiently.

"That shows that Mr Hammond only arrived after the murder. As he found the body, he put down the miniatures at once, but over the still moist bloodstains."

Now I understood the importance of this observation. I spoke out: "But that is wonderful. You can demonstrate Hammond's innocence. Are you going to tell Professor Hammond?"

"No, Watson, I do not intend to do that just yet." I looked at him in surprise.

"Before Monday I can do nothing for him through the official channels, and he and his uncle would have to curb their impatience. But there is something else. I am particularly preoccupied with the curious behaviour of Dr. Miller. There is something there which for which I still have to find an explanation."

It suddenly struck me that Porky had yesterday referred to him in just the same way. I now knew where we were going, for the address was that of the house of Dr. and Mrs. Miller.

It seemed to me rather unfeeling, that we should trouble Mrs. Miller, so newly a widow, only days after the tragic death of her husband. Holmes however saw it as a necessity, so I was now there to accompany him. A few minutes later we were in the study at the Miller household, waiting for a conversation with his widow. I took my place at a small table, in the centre of the room, reflecting, how best to express my sympathy. Holmes however walked up and down between me and the fireplace.

As Mrs. Miller entered, my fear that we were much out of place became certainty. Under her black dress, there were the unmistakeable signs for me that she was in an advanced stage of pregnancy. It would be wiser for her at this time to be spared any anxiety or burden, and yet she had now to bear the loss of her husband. The grief and burden were obvious in her face. I looked warningly at Holmes, and wondered whether the circumstances might be as clear to him.

After we had expressed our sympathy over Dr. Miller's death, she asked us to put our questions briefly, because she could not give us much time. That seemed understandable. Holmes began gently to explain that we were trying to exonerate Brian Hammond from the murder for which he was now in prison. It was the best way to start, for Mrs Miller at once said that she could not believe that Hammond was a murderer. She had hardly known him, but her husband had been so full of praise for him, and she had been impressed. Holmes had at first avoided a direct question concerning Dr. Miller, but now he must.

"Please, Mrs. Miller, help me if you can. It is important to know the truth about Mr. Hammond and his work. He told us that he felt Dr. Miller was unusually nervous during the recovery and shipment of the excavation treasures. Can you perhaps confirm that?"

There was a pause before she answered. "Yes, Mr. Holmes, it was so. You must understand that as soon as I knew I was carrying our child, I felt a happy, a wonderful time opening up for me.

"Vincent seemed, however, uneasy, as if he could not come to terms with it. He was permanently nervous and irritated. I scarcely could recognise the man I had married. He went out almost every evening, and came home late. He preferred to spend his nights here on the couch in this study, rather than with me. He said he didn't want to disturb me, but I could not sleep, knowing that he was out at night."

The tears could not be stemmed, and she paused before wiping her eyes and again became calm. She continued quietly, that Vincent had truly loved his work, and that she had hoped the recovery of the burial chamber would bring the satisfaction he perhaps needed. But she followed: "But no, he was worse than ever. Now he was angry with everybody and everything, and I was even afraid of him. Indeed, I was more at ease when he slept here.

"I am very sorry, gentlemen, but I must ask you to leave me now. I am departing this evening to be taken to my father, who lives not far from here, to stay with him until the birth. All is ready, and I will be leaving soon, when the carriage comes, so as to make the journey in daylight".

We naturally took our leave at once, thanking her for the help she had given us, and left this house of mourning.

Outside in the street, I observed that Holmes was not as impatient as usual to find a cab and return home. He seemed more concerned with walking, and set off briskly, to satisfy, as I thought, his need of fresh air and exercise. We walked some way in silence, both of us occupied with our thoughts about this newest experience. Both with the Thames Murders, and the Secret of the Three Monks, I had the privilege of seeing that his heart was at least as great and generous as that more obvious aspect, which everyone praised, of his clear and incisive intellect. Here, however, nothing of this seemed to concern him. I was truly disappointed only to experience the cold-blooded logical and intellectual person which Holmes could be. It was just in this moment that Holmes spoke to me.

"What would you say to dinner at Simpsons, Watson?"

I tried to conceal my disappointment at what seemed yet another example of unfeeling heartlessness. "Certainly, Holmes"

"If you don't mind, I would be pleased if we could walk there," he said suddenly.

I nodded. I became aware that Holmes was looking at me, and some moments elapsed before he spoke again.

"I will only remain with you at Simpsons until half past nine. You will please find your own way back to Baker Street."

"Have you another appointment?" I asked, surprised.

"Well, you might indeed call it that," he replied smiling. "I am going back to Lexington Street."

"But Holmes, you know that Mrs. Miller will no longer be there. She was about to leave to go to her father's house. And if you want to talk to the house staff, would that not be done better tomorrow morning? They will, when you get there, surely no longer be on duty."

"Indeed, that is what I am hoping," replied Holmes with a smile. I was now truly confused and irritated. I had the feeling that he was making fun at my expense. I expressed my impatience.

"Come on, Holmes, what are you doing?"

He looked at me and spoke as indifferently as if he were discussing the weather. "I am going to break into the house."

I stopped abruptly, and stared at him. He stood there before me and seemed to be amused by my consternation.

"You are doing what?" I stammered.

"Breaking in, my friend. Something there in Dr. Miller's study caught my attention, and aroused my curiosity."

"And what was that?"

"I will explain it all, but now we must walk on, or we may fail to obtain a table for dinner."

He set off again briskly, and I could only follow his example.

"Now, Holmes, please explain to me what it was that caught your attention", I asked.

"The carpet under the small table at which you were sitting".

Before I could say more, he continued, "I saw that

1. The carpet had a particularly fine pattern, but this was scarcely visible where the carpet lies at present; both the chair and the table are standing on it.
2. The carpet had on one side a few visible burns. These are quite characteristic for the sparks which sometimes fall from a wood fire, burning in an open fireplace. In Dr. Miller's study, however, the fireplace is some fifteen feet away from the carpet as it lies now. The sparks cannot fly so far; the carpet was originally much nearer the fireplace.

"Why, now, I ask myself, should such a handsome carpet, which certainly was intended to be in front of the fireplace, where it would be much more effective, now lie in such an unsuitable place?"

Holmes saw my helplessness. "Why, because it is now being used to hide something! I suspect that under it there are loose boards. What they might conceal, I will tonight try to find out."

"But Holmes, must you really break in to find that out? Could you not have asked Mrs. Miller directly? She would have shown it to you."

Holmes did not answer at once, but a smile spread over his face.

"My dear Watson, you were earlier still troubled that I wanted to speak at all with Mrs. Miller. Now you are asking me why, directly in the presence of his widow, I did not do something which, if successful, might severely harm his good name. And do not try to suggest that there is probably nothing there. I was not ready to take that risk in the presence of Mrs. Miller. No, what I now find, if anything, only I will have found. Apart from my own conscience, I have to give account to nobody about my actions. Expressed another way, if I think it right, I can even suppress any evidence I may find, as long as no-one else suffers from my doing so."

As he was saying this, he had become more agitated, and I could well understand why. I had made him aware of my concern, even of my misgivings, about his apparent lack of feeling, whereas in truth he had the whole time been concerned to avoid unnecessary harm and protect innocent parties from hurt. In this not only Dr. Miller and his reputation were concerned, but also Brian Hammond. Why had I not seen this for myself? It hurt me to think that I had misjudged my old friend. I took his arm and stopped again, thus obliging him also to stop. Then I spoke.

"Holmes, I must apologise to you. I thought you were only concerned with facts and evidence, and that you were not concerned with the persons involved. That was an error, and I see now clearly how you are determined to protect them all. Please forgive me."

"I assure you, Watson, that there is nothing to forgive. You have, as a result of your restricted view of the various factors, simply arrived at a false conclusion. I have to admit that if I had been able to involve you more, in my process of deduction, that might not have happened. But you also understand my methods, and you know that unless I am sure of a conclusion, I cannot talk about it. You see, then, that you need no longer let your head hang, my friend. All is well."

He turned to me again to put his arm round me, and I felt at once greatly relieved, for I knew that he avoided whenever he could any gesture of emotion. We could thus go on our way reassured.

Dinner at Simpson's was as always excellent, and we concluded with a whisky and a cigar. Holmes told me something of cases I had not known, such as the Trepoff murder in Odessa, and the Atkinson tragedy. At around half past nine, he called for the bill, and prepared to leave me. I, however, laid a hand on his arm, and asked if I might accompany him. His expression showed his pleasure, but also his concern.

"My dear Watson, I would greatly value your company, but please think of the consequences. What I am planning to do, even though it serves a noble end, is, in the eyes of the law, a criminal act. You, however, my friend, are no longer going through life alone, but have also to think of your responsibility to your good lady."

"Of that, Holmes, I am well aware, but I am still prepared to accompany you." I was quite sure of what I was saying, and indeed, of the possible consequences of our actions. But I could not do otherwise. The bond of friendship which linked me to Holmes was, beside Mary, at the heart of my being. I saw the expression on his face as we stood up, left the restaurant, and set off together.

The villa in Lexington Street was now, as we arrived, in complete darkness. Holmes drew out of his jacket pocket a small leather purse, in which he had a number of small bright metal tools. I looked nervously up and down the street. It was only a matter of moments for him to open the heavy front door. He really would have made a very successful burglar. I had the passing thought, as at other times, that it was well for London that he had not chosen to embark on a life of crime.

Once inside we followed the way into the study as in the afternoon. Holmes led me so that I would not stumble over any obstacles in the darkness. Once in the study, there was a little light as the moon fell rather thinly upon the windows of the double doors to the garden. It was not much, indeed, but it was enough to illuminate our work. Table, chairs and carpet were quickly moved aside, and Holmes, on hands and knees, felt with his fingertips the bare boards underneath. Suddenly he looked up and I saw the smile on his face. He took his pocket-knife and lifted carefully a floor panel. In the space beneath it he felt a round hole. He lit a match, and looked into the hole. As the match died out, he reached down and lifted up a wallet of papers. Just in this moment, however, we heard movement over our heads. There were footsteps.

The panel was at once replaced, carpet, chairs and table were brought back. It was already almost too late, for the gas light in the hallway was already lit, shining under the door. That way out was already impossible. Holmes went quickly to the double door window, and with his tools at once released the lock. I grabbed the wallet, and we were in a moment in the garden. I was about to run, but Holmes caught me and pressed me against the house wall, while he closed and locked the door behind him. Sure enough, and a few moments later, the gas light came on in the study. Had I run, I risked being seen. We heard a rattle as the person inside tested the double doors and saw that they were locked, and then all was quiet, and the study was again dark. We waited a moment, and then ran through the garden, to the wall surrounding it. I thought I could climb it, but seen from nearer it was too high. Holmes, ahead of me, said, "Don't worry, Watson, I'll help you".

At the wall, I put down the wallet, and Holmes formed his hands to create a stirrup for me. I climbed up as best I could, and sat astride the wall. Holmes then gave me the wallet, and

I caught it securely. Now it was his turn, and he took a few steps back while I stretched my arm down. He took a running jump, caught his hands on the top of the wall, with his feet scratching on the wall, before I could catch hold of him to pull him further up. Soon he too was astride the wall. We looked at one another like schoolboys. He then slipped gracefully down to land on his feet. I now threw down the wallet to him. My descent was certainly less catlike and elegant, but we were now safely on the pavement in Marshall Street, where at this time there was nobody to observe us. Very relieved, we set about walking back to Baker Street.

A Skytala

As soon as we were safely back in Baker Street, we sat down at the round dining table, to look at the contents of the wallet. We agreed to work systematically, in a fixed plan, so that Holmes took first an item, and then, after looking at it, passed it to me. The first paper was a letter from Cox's Bank. The letter was three months old and was clearly a reply to an enquiry of Dr Miller. It informed him that without prior consultation with his wife, there could be no discussion on the subject of a mortgage. There followed letters from other banks which were in content almost identical. The tenor in each case was that he could be offered credit, but in view of the sum proposed, he would be required to offer an adequate security. Then followed a sealing stamp such as is used in endorsing the seal on a letter or package. It had the initials V.M. Both the grip, and also the seal itself, were completely without ornament, which meant that it suggested nothing.

Given the ornamentation of the study, this surprised me a little. Further searching produced a letter without sender's address, containing a short message and the half of a pledge for debt. This, for fifty pounds, was signed by Dr. Miller. The short note said only, *I am in possession of all your promissory notes for your debts. Come at once to the Bar of Gold Club.* Then there were in the wallet various newspaper cuttings, in which loans were offered, and older gambling receipts. These were all over three years old. I thumbed through these without particular intention, while Holmes studied the anonymous note.

"It looks as if Porky's information about the promissory notes was in fact quite correct," he said, continuing thoughtfully, "Obviously Dr. Miller had accumulated large gambling debts, and was now desperately trying to pay them off. The promissory notes and pledges were, as Porky had suggested, already for several weeks in the hands of another person. That meant that this person could now exercise his power over Dr. Miller to blackmail him".

"Then the question must be, who is this person?" I asked.

"I fear that I can already answer that question", said Holmes.

I looked at him rather surprised, but as if speaking his thoughts aloud he carried on, "What the Diogenes Club is to my brother Mycroft, the Bar of Gold Club is for Colonel Sebastian Moran".

The mention of this name was enough to make my heart beat quicker. In Holmes' criminal files, Colonel Moran occupied the second place. He came only second to Professor Moriarty, whose adjutant and deputy he was. Professor Moriarty was, in Holmes' eyes, the Napoleon of crime and his bitterest opponent. However, he had never been charged or accused directly of any misdemeanour, and in everyday affairs he continued to live the life of a modest and harmless professor of mathematics.

As I recovered from my first shock, I asked, "Holmes, do you think then that Professor Moriarty is in some way involved in all this?"

"Very possibly, Watson. Yet it is not clear to me, how a connection might exist. After all, with all respect to Dr. Miller, how could he have been of any value to the villainous mind of Professor Moriarty? Dr. Miller was an archaeologist with special interest in Egyptology, and as such an employee at the British Museum. He spent most of his time there, although there would occasionally be excavations in which he took part. There was little else. I wonder how that could interest Professor Moriarty."

I followed Holmes' muttered words with a nod and continued to sift rather absently through the newspaper cuttings. Holmes' hand suddenly fell across my papers. Alarmed, I looked up to see that his face was almost white, lined with his concentration. He held up a small strip of paper, which he had pulled out from between the other papers.

"Holmes, is something not in order?" I asked. He reacted not in the least, but searched all around, and suddenly seemed to find what he wanted. His other hand flew across the table to snatch up the sealing stamp. He held his breath and, with unsteady fingers, wrapped the short strip of paper around the handle of the stamp. As soon as that was done, he held the stamp in both hands and rolled it between his fingers. His eyes burned with excitement, and I heard him breathing heavily.

"Oh, Watson, how could I have been so blind! I was indeed blind. But now I have the key. This is a Skytala, a Skytala!"

As he said this, he spun round and held the sealing stamp close to his heart. This behaviour was so completely out of character that it was for me a complete surprise. But then, as quickly as he had given vent to his delight, as quickly again he returned to me to stand upright, still and concentrating. He stared into empty space, but as quickly smiled and fell on his knees before the fireplace. I followed him, and saw how his one hand grasped the stamp, while his other sifted through the grate and the cold ashes.

"Holmes, what is it?" I cried, but he gave no sign of response. He stood up, put the stamp in his pocket and hunted through his writing desk. There were so many papers, and they landed haphazardly on the floor. Now he went to the bookcase, pulling out books, shaking them and letting them fall. I wanted to calm him, but all I heard was, "Where is it then?"

If my doctor's bag had been beside me I could have tried something to calm him, but now Mrs. Hudson had been awaked by the noise, and appeared in the doorway, in her nightgown, with a blanket round her shoulders, and her nightcap on her head. She could not avoid a shrill scream as she saw the chaos which Holmes had already caused. Her shout seemed however to break through into Holmes' thoughts, as he turned on his heel and came to her.

Outright, without ceremony, he asked, "Where are the papers that I threw into the fireplace?" Puzzled and stunned, she could only reply, "I put them in my zinc bucket as I always do with the old papers. I use them to light my kitchen fire, Mr. Holmes."

Instantly Holmes drew back, away from her, and ran down the stairs to the kitchen. Mrs. Hudson and I exchanged an alarmed look, before we ran to the stairs to follow him.

We found the kitchen floor already taking on the same disorder as the carpet upstairs, with Holmes crawling about on all fours among the scraps and papers which he had abruptly tipped out of the bin. Suddenly his hand shot out in front of him, and he held up in triumph a scrap of paper, similar to that he had found in Dr. Miller's wallet. He then took the stamp from his pocket, and just as upstairs, hastened to wind the paper strip around the handle of the stamp. A broad smile came to his lips, but then froze again as he asked me, apparently in no coherent sense, "Watson, when does the museum's exhibition of the grave chamber open?"

Surprised, I answered, "Why, it is to be opened tomorrow morning."

"Then there is no more time to lose. I only hope we are not already too late. Watson, do you have your revolver there?" He tore a page out of his notebook and wrote a few lines quickly. I was still too confused to answer, but nodded to reassure him. He continued in a firm and energetic voice.

"Good, Watson, you may need it. And Mrs. Hudson, you will please bring this note directly to my brother, Mycroft: Here is the address. I know it is night-time, but do not let yourself be turned away. He must read this and act at once upon it. Watson's life and mine will depend upon it."

Mrs. Watson was nothing if courageous. "Mr. Holmes", she answered, suddenly quite determined, "Just let me dress and I will leave at once. And please do not worry about me." She hastened out of the room and went to her bedroom.

I fetched my revolver and, once we were in our street clothes, we set off at once, in haste, out of the house, into Baker Street and to the street corner. There, to our relief, was a hackney, the driver no doubt expecting to go home to rest. He stopped for us, and Holmes gave him the address of the British Museum.

Now I could ask him. "Holmes, just what does all this mean?"

"I will explain it all, but did you ever read my monograph on codes and cyphers?" He had caught me.

"I'm sorry, Holmes, no, I have not".

"Then let me explain briefly the background in a huge field. There are two kinds of coding, the monoalphabetic coding often called Substitution, and the practice known as Transposition. In the first, every letter is represented by another letter. There are well-known models such as the so-called Caesar-numbering, which allows by means of a number disc that every text can be coded and then decoded by simple procedure. In the Transposition code, letters retain their meaning but are subject to a different order in the text. These two forms may also be combined, which makes it extremely difficult to break them, unless one has the key. Nevertheless, it is possible, by laborious testing, and with knowledge of the normal frequencies with which letters occur in use, to decode them."

I was tired and nervous, and could still not work out what it was that Holmes was telling me. I interrupted Holmes to say, "That is surely most interesting, but what has it to do with our case? Is there a coded secret message?"

"Oh, yes, Watson, we have two of them. The first I found in Dr. Miller's papers. The message is on this piece of paper."

He handed me the narrow paper strip, and I looked at it. The following letters were written on it in capital letters:

EM REOCL XMH RNEO PEAOSSSW EDNF E CID OQF TAOPRUO TVA EL IEEPCN

It seemed strangely familiar to me, and suddenly I realised where I had seen something like it before.

"Holmes, the strip of paper which you had from Mycroft, the scrap which was in the mouth of the consular employee in Cairo when he died, was that the other one?"

"Exactly, Watson! Now you understand, why, after I had found the one message, I had really to find the other!"

I understood. "Of course, Holmes, but now, what do the messages tell us?"

"That you will soon see, my friend, but first let me tell you another method of coding."

That puzzled me. "But surely you just said that there were two methods, which you just explained."

"Excellent, Watson, I see that as always, you not only listen, but think about what it means. Yes, you are quite right, and I now explain a type of transposition. And yet, this method is completely unique. It was in use at least two and a half thousand years ago, and that has given it the name 'The Spartan Skytala.' Skytala is a Greek word for a stick or staff. The military leadership of Sparta used it to transmit secret information within their army. To transmit, and then have access, to the information, the sender and the recipient must each have a so-called Skytala. These are cylinders of the same radius. And this is how it works. A band of parchment is wrapped around the cylinder of the sender. The message is then written along the staff. When the message has to be read, the band must be wrapped similarly around the identical staff of the recipient.

"You see therefore that the coding of a message with Skytala is simple, but offers high security. For a criminal network such as is led by Professor Moriarty, this may be very practical. But now try yourself to decode the messages: first, the one which we found in Dr. Miller's papers."

With these words Holmes gave me the strip of paper and the sealing stamp whose grip had obviously served as a Skytala. I wound the strip around the grip. As soon as I turned it around in my hand, and even in the dim light of the small lamp in the cab, I was able to read this message:

EXPECT IMMEDIATE HANDOVER OF PAPERS OR CONSEQUENCES FOLLOW

Astonished, I looked at Holmes and asked the critical question,

"Do you know what papers are here intended?"

"Read the next message, and I wager, you will answer that yourself ".

As he spoke, he gave me the second strip of paper, and I wrapped this around our Skytala. This gave the following message:

GIVE PAPERS TO DR MILLER AT 12 IN EL FISCHAWI

"Holmes, I am not quite sure, but I seem to recall that El Fischawi is one of Cairo's best-known coffee houses."

"Yes, Watson, you are quite right, it is in the great Bazaar, Khan el Kahalili."

It struck me like a blow. "Holmes, we are talking here of the stolen secret plans of the Suez Canal!"

"Brilliant, Watson, you see how all the pieces of the puzzle are now dropping into their places. The consular clerk,

Edward Parker, under the orders of Professor Moriarty, stole the secret papers, and gave them, as instructed to Dr. Miller in the Café El Fischawi. Dr. Miller was, as a result of his gambling debts, already working for Professor Moriarty. Since he could not know when the theft might take place, Dr. Miller had stayed in his hotel room in Cairo, awaiting instructions, when he should have been ordering the packing and loading of the contents of the tomb which he had excavated. Once he had received the papers, he was then able to conceal them in one of the packing cases being prepared for loading on the ship."

Holmes paused, and I found myself dreaming. I had before me the image of Dr. Miller, hurrying through the narrow streets of Cairo, which I had seen on my voyage to India, years before. He would pick his way through unpaved alleyways, full of all kinds of refuse and which, in the heat, were often damp and evil-smelling. Many were so narrow that two riders could not pass; the overhanging eaves and balconies almost touch one another. I saw Dr. Miller picking his way between people and their beasts, some carrying goatskins of water or other goods, some with donkeys, and some with handcarts or wagons of goods. Then there was the noise, whips cracking, camels and donkeys protesting, shouts of the drivers, beggars crying out, and still others at prayer. I was surely tired, but through this fantasy came the steady voice of Holmes, so that I was back with him in the cab.

"When the SS Bokhara docked in London, Dr. Miller surely wanted to recover the papers at the first opportunity, for time was already short and the messages had suggested threats.

Perhaps we will never know what he intended exactly to do, but he was there at the dockside, obviously nervous and careless. The consequence, however it occurred, was the fatal accident. Professor Moriarty knew that the papers were to be transported in the packing cases, but could not know which, and so he sent his hired thief to break into the museum and search for them. This was the end of Peter Shephard, for he discovered the thief, and was murdered."

Holmes paused again, and I thought where his remarks were leading us. "So we are on the way, here in the dead of night, to the British Museum, where you think the papers are still somewhere concealed? But the grave chamber crates have all been unpacked. Would not one of the museum employees have seen the papers and aroused suspicion?"

"I think, Watson, we have to think rather more carefully. These crates and their contents have been thoroughly examined by customs and police first in Egypt, and then here in London. Dr. Miller knew that he could not simply drop the papers in with the grave goods. No, he had to hide them much more carefully, very carefully indeed. And I think I know where that might be." I waited, impatiently.

"I think they are concealed inside the mummy! That would be the smartest place, safe and dry, and yet protected by superstition and even disgust from any kind of interference."

It was an astonishing thought, and I was admittedly shocked. I found the thought of opening up a corpse which had been embalmed thousands of years ago, distinctly uninviting. But I could ask no more, for we were already at the British Museum.

The Exhibition Hall

As we climbed the steps to the great main entrance, I confess I was suddenly taken aback by the enormity of our undertaking. Should we not wait until the police arrived, as they would do, as soon as Mycroft had given the alarm? Or should we have alerted the Museum Director, Lord Armstrong, that we intended to break into the Museum and perhaps damage the mummy? All these wild thoughts were banished, however, as we saw that the door had already been damaged and forced. Holmes looked at me in alarm, and whispered,

"This must have been done by Moriarty's people. The question will be, have they already found the papers, or not? I think they will first seek to silence the watchmen, so as to search without being disturbed." I hoped that he was right.

When we reached the dark entrance hall, it seemed that this suspicion was justified. We could see a man lying on the floor. From closer it was apparent that he was the watchman here. I knelt beside him and could establish with relief that he lived. He had been hit, hard, and then very professionally bound. I would have released him, but Holmes whispered urgently, "No! We can do that later. For the moment we don't know where they are, but they also do not know that we are here. Let us keep this status quo as long as possible."

I nodded, and then whispered, "The exhibition is on the first floor."

"Then that is where we must go," said Holmes, seizing the dark lantern which was beside the watchman, and setting off up the stairs, with all caution.

Without a sound we climbed up the great marble staircase, as quickly as we could. The exhibition hall was in complete darkness, and we entered it very cautiously. Holmes, as soon as he was sure we were alone, opened the shutter of the lantern, just enough to allow a faint yellow light to fall upon the exhibits. We were suddenly aware of the monumental scale of the exhibition, and the number of items around us, which, together with the great sailcloth drapes and in the faint light, gave the impression that we really were in a burial chamber deep in the heart of an Egyptian pyramid.

We were for a moment almost overawed with the scale and drama of this scene. Now we could see the glass shrine in which the mummy was exhibited. The lid of the sarcophagus had been lifted aside, and stood vertically at the side. The mummy was now open to view. Holmes looked carefully at the lock on the glass shrine. A triumphant smile came to his face as he turned to me, gave me the lantern to hold and said, "The lock is intact. Moriarty's people have not yet been here".

That seemed good news, but knowing that they were in the museum and could at any moment appear, I was distinctly uncomfortable. Holmes produced his small leather wallet of tools, and set to work, as I held the lantern. Less than a minute sufficed to release the lock, the glass door swung open, and Holmes entered the glass shrine. Carefully he lifted the mummy out of the sarcophagus, and laid it on the floor. He knelt beside it.

"Watson, please hold the lantern over my hands," he whispered. I did as he said, and saw how his hands moved gently over the body from head to foot. Then he turned the mummy over, and did the same over the back. Near the middle of the back, he stopped abruptly, and muttered urgently, "More light!" I followed his wish, and saw how he took out his pocket knife. Just where he had stopped with his hand, he plunged it deep into the mummy. With the blade, he opened the hole to a slit, about six inches long. I was surprised, how easy this was. Now he put the knife aside, and slipped his hand into the slit.

I have to admit to being relieved that I only had to hold the lantern. I found the prospect of searching around in an embalmed and bandaged corpse anything but inviting. But then Holmes withdrew his hand, slowly and carefully, and I saw that he held a thick package in his hand. There rose from his hand, and from the package, a not disagreeable scent of oils and herbs. Holmes allowed himself one quick look, and then said, "These are the Suez Canal papers. Now we must see that we get out of here quickly." He stuffed the whole package into an inside jacket pocket.

At that moment I became aware of movement. Without hesitating, I threw myself over him and knocked him to the floor. I threw the lantern as far away from us as possible. I heard several shots, and something clattered as it was hit. Holmes und I knelt between the shrine and the mummy, at least partly covered by the heavy stone sarcophagus. I lifted my own revolver up and as soon as I felt movement, fired a shot. When two rounds were left, I turned to Holmes, but he said, "I know, Watson, you have only two more rounds, and our situation appears already hopeless. But even if we have lost this game, the match is not yet over."

Holmes' words warmed me. If he, with his rational approach, found there was still hope, then it was not yet time to give up. Just at that moment more shots were fired. Some struck the glass shrine, already cracked and starred. It collapsed with a crash and a rain of glass splinters, and as I instinctively fired back my last two shots they were followed by a complete silence. It was broken by an ice-cold and scornful voice.

"I think, gentlemen, that it is time to give up."

I looked questioningly at Holmes, who whispered, "That is Colonel Moran. Do not let him provoke you. He takes a pleasure in tormenting people and killing them."

We stood up, and were immediately surrounded by eight armed men. Demonstratively, I let my revolver fall. A large, powerful-looking man stepped forward from the circle. He walked up to us, a contemptuous grin on his face, while his cold fish-like eyes searched us without sign of emotion.

"If you please, I will now take the papers".

He reached out a hand to Holmes. Carefully, Holmes took the package from his inside pocket, and handed it to Colonel Moran.

"Thank you, Mr Holmes. You have spared us the search for the papers. I admit that I would not have thought so readily that the mummy would itself be the hiding place. It is clearly very true that, as the Professor says, you have a very clever brain."

He hesitated and observed Holmes. My friend however only stood and looked at him. Moran continued. "You have indeed often disturbed our business affairs, but this time you will have no chance to interfere. This night, the Professor will give the papers to 'Pierrot,' and in the morning they will leave the country." He waited for a reaction. There came none.

"You are very quiet, Mr. Holmes. I feel that you are not quite so satisfied with your present role on the losing side. Surely you know, such a clever thinker as you are, that you must ultimately fail?" There was another pause.

"The organisation which our Professor leads must succeed over all others, because our values are power, influence, possessions and wealth, which will always triumph! Just look at the absurd values which you represent, and for which you are ready even to die: a good reputation, honesty, justice and friendship".

At this point he broke out into loud laughter, and his henchmen did likewise. The insulting talk of the Colonel had injured my sense of honour, as he had drawn down into the dirt all that which was noble in Holmes' life and work. I would have fallen upon him, but my glance at Holmes told me to keep control of my feelings and give no sign of provocation. Holmes was breathing heavily, and faster, and his fists were clenched, his knuckles white, but his face still showed an unmoved expression. If Holmes could so control himself, then I must too, even though it might be as much as I could do.

"Now, Mr. Holmes, what shall we do with you and your friend? If it were left to me, then…."

He did not complete the sentence, but his meaning was obvious enough. So he continued: "That would not be what the Professor wants. He is curiously occupied in looking forward to a future confrontation of your intelligence with his. I have to take you downstairs and lock you in the cellars." There broke out another wave of demonic laughter, and the others joined in.

Prisoners

With so many of Colonel Moran's men around us, there could be no thought of flight. We descended to the vaulted cellar, and from there into a side room, while the Colonel and four men remained by the stairs. We had not been disturbed by watchmen, so perhaps they had all been disabled and bound. Now came two more of the band, each with a can of petroleum, which they sprinkled over the floor and the stored objects.

Colonel Moran spoke to us again, in a curiously affected voice. "You see, my friends, that I have, as Professor Moriarty ordered, done you no harm. Regrettably, however, in your attempt to escape you have caused a fire to break out in the cellar."

With this he took a cloth from his pocket, soaked it also in the petroleum, and, with a match, set it alight. He threw the burning cloth quickly from himself, onto a few hemp sacks lying on one side. He laughed, again, scornfully. He turned on his heel, and closed the door, and we heard the key turn. His vicious laughter still rang in my ears. I looked at Holmes, who thought for a moment.

"These cellars are a labyrinth and our hope must be that there is another way out somewhere. Perhaps we will find a window without bars."

We walked briskly away from the fire, which was rapidly gaining hold. I followed him, and the occasional windows let in some light from the London night sky. We found no way out, and the only hope seemed to be a crowbar, perhaps used for opening packing cases, which Holmes picked up and took with him. We walked further and further, but then we came to a wall which closed our way. Holmes suggested that we had reached the end of the building, and that the cellars went no further. His sense of direction told him we should be at the northwest façade, and that we were at the point furthest removed from the fire. Typically, he was still thinking coolly and analytically about our choices. He said to me, "Before the fire and smoke reach us, we may have a little time. I propose to try to free the grill before this window from the stonework in which it is anchored"

With the crowbar he shattered the glass, and then attacked the cement which secured the bars. After a few heavy blows, he began to perspire, and took off his jacket and waistcoat, finally rolling up his sleeves. Then he again set to work. I saw as before, what strength he put into his blows with the crowbar. I found myself speculating helplessly, whether my shoulder, so maltreated in Afghanistan, could be any use. I took off my jacket and prepared to do my best. Holmes stopped for breath, and said nothing. His expression, told me what he was thinking. Even if we could do it, it would take a long time, time which we obviously did not have.

I set to work, ignoring the pain in my shoulder, and hammered on the cement filling, until I could really do no more. I gave Holmes the crowbar and he set to again with full force. As I watched I remembered somewhere that I had seen a block and tackle, used for lifting the heavy crates and objects. I had paid it no attention, as so much was lying around, but now it seemed to offer a first sign of rescue. I told Holmes.

"It must surely help, Watson. Where did you see it?"

"It was hanging in the half-light as we came through to here. I would know the place if I see it."

"Yes", said Holmes, "But you cannot go back toward the fire."

"Holmes, I will not go near the fire. I should be back inside five minutes". He was obviously not convinced, but what should we do? He wanted to come with me, but if we did not find it and were away longer, there was even less chance to break out. He had to accept the fact that I would go back and search. Our roles were clear.

"In order, Watson, but be careful. He set to work again.

I went at once, and within five minutes had reached the place where I had seen the block and tackle. It hung on a hook in the cellar ceiling. I looked in vain for a ladder to reach it, but then realised that there was here an empty cabinet, free of exhibits. If I could climb on it, I would be near enough to lean over and lift it free from its hook. Clearly it was a risk, but we needed the block and tackle and there was no time to lose.

I climbed up, and stood on top of the cabinet. It was not very stable, but I could at least reach out, and I caught the shackle which held the tackle on the hook. Then by an effort I lifted it off the hook. I had it! I swung it over my shoulder to climb down. But I had ignored the weight which now shifted my balance, so that I stepped backwards, and I could do no more to prevent myself from falling to the floor. As I fell, I held my breath, and I felt that I had landed on a pile of sacking, which was softer that the stone floor. Then, however, I knew no more, as all went dark.

I could not say how long I lay there, but I awoke coughing. The air was smoky, and breathing was difficult. Tears rolled from my eyes. I sat up as best I could, and noted almost without thinking, that my ribs and chest seemed undamaged. I tried to move my legs, and they followed my thoughts; at least there was no serious injury. I had surely a few bruises and scratches, and my head was very painful. Trying to stand, I was at once dizzy, and I had to vomit a time or two. Everything seemed to spin around me, cold sweat broke out and I knew my blood pressure was low. My heart was hammering. I slid down the wall to sit on the floor. Feeling behind my head, I found blood and an egg-sized swelling. I must have hit my head on an object as I fell. Concussion, said the doctor in me, immediate rest. In panic I found myself laughing at the self-diagnosis.

I realised slowly that I had to get out of this place, but how? I could neither stand nor walk. I tried on hands and knees. It was not good, but I came away from that place, pulling the block and tackle behind me like a trophy. After a few feet, I was exhausted. I lay on the ground, and the smoke again burned in my lungs. I wanted to stay here and sleep. It was then that my beloved Mary appeared in my inner vision, stretching out a hand to me and calling my name. Was it this that gave me new strength? I struggled again onto hands and knees, and I found a little strength to move again, ten feet, twenty feet, twenty five feet, but no, it was no use, my strength failed completely. There was no air, no oxygen. My eyes filled with tears, and indescribable sadness, and I closed my eyes knowing it was the last time.

I knew nothing more, but pictures started to flicker in my mind, as from a magic lantern, at first scenes of beauty, happy times with Mary and Holmes. Then the scene changed, and the nightmare of my military experiences in Afghanistan filled my inner view. At last I saw idyllic and innocent pictures of my childhood, with my brother, and with our parents. But why was I now in a tunnel, dark and frightening? At the end appeared a warm, incredibly welcoming light, I had only to go towards it. I was nearly there, when the image was shattered. A huge bird hovered and circled, shrieking, over me. It was a great falcon, and it carried something on its head. At once I knew that this was the Horus-Falcon with the double crown of Egypt, of which Lord Armstrong had told me. I wanted to get to the light, but I could not. The falcon fell on me and I felt its fangs in my arm. The creature had such strength that it drew me back again, away from the warm, comforting light. I fell once again into darkness.

There came to me a sensation of being shaken, and of my face being slapped. I opened my eyes and blinked. Over me I saw Holmes' pale and deeply anxious face.

"Thank Heaven! Watson, you are still alive!" And then I heard his deep sigh, as he breathed his relief. I was truly not less surprised to see his face once more again in this life. In my effort to speak, my voice failed me.

"Quiet, Watson, quiet. You must lie still. I will get us out of here, with your tackle."

What was that? Tackle? I saw him take up the block and tackle I had found, and secure it to the ceiling. Slowly and only now I began to realise where I was. It was the room at the end of the cellar, where I had left him. From where I lay, I could now see that he had done a thorough job, and had broken out some of the cement, leaving the bars partly free. I saw Holmes now take the end of the rope and secure it to the barred grille. Now he took the other end, and, pulled with all his might. The line tightened and the block and tackle gave off a tormented sound. I could see how cracks had opened in the cement, and tried to see better. My voice came back.

"You can do it! My God, Holmes, you can do it".

He came no further, and took a short break, struggling for breath. My heart was beating fast as I watched him. He was covered in dust, but I saw his face white and bloodless. Sweat stood out on his face, and ran over his cheeks. His white shirt was grey with dust and sweat, clinging to his body. I saw his breast rising and falling, and heard his heavy breathing. I saw then his hands, and realised that they were covered in blood. He had obviously worked with the crowbar, until they were raw and torn, and now the heavy rough rope was opening up the wounds again. I knew of old his iron constitution, and his tremendous willpower, but I feared that he was here close to the limit.

After struggling with the crowbar, he had come to rescue me, and had surely inhaled the biting smoke where I lay. He had then carried me back to the end of the cellar, and was now fighting his exhaustion and pain to set us free. As these thoughts filled me, he took up the end of the rope, and made to pull it again. I had an appalling pain in my head, and yet I still tried to sit up. Then I tried to stand. The urge to vomit came back, but I held it back. I shuffled nearer to Holmes, and caught the end of the rope. I pulled it with my last force, as hard as I could. My legs gave way, and I fell again to the floor, but I did not relax my grip and my weight still pulled on the rope.

Holmes saw my hands below his, and for a moment he smiled, his eyes warming as he realised I was there. Then, as I fell again to the floor, I saw how his jaw set, and the eyes screwed up in concentration, as he made a last seemingly impossible, superhuman effort. The cracks in the cement widened and then, with a loud crack, the barred grille fell to the floor. We were free.

I felt how Holmes helped me to my feet, and pulled me to a packing case under the window. He lifted me up, and pushed me out through the window. I felt under my hands the gravel surrounding the building, and crawled a few inches more to make room for Holmes. I saw how he rolled to one side and then found his way out beside me. We lay side by side and stared at one another. Our lungs drew in the fresh air, while our hearts, beating like a drumroll, gradually slowed down and found their rhythm. It had been a close-run thing, but we had done it.

Slowly, as we calmed down, we heard noises in the distance, apparently approaching us as they became louder. It took time before we could say what noises they were, but then I heard horses' hooves, the sound of wheels on the gravel, and a confusion of voices. Holmes smiled thinly at me and said, "Watson, that sounds like the cavalry! I must let them know we are here!"

"Holmes, if you can support me, let me come with you."

"Very good, Watson, then we shall go together".

He stood up slowly, and then helped me to my feet. He took my left arm and laid it over his shoulder. His still iron grip held my left wrist, and his right arm now went around my waist. We reached the frontage of the building and we saw a whole company of men, and some horses, taking up their work. Many of them were from the fire brigade, tackling the fire in the cellar.

Two men however were watching out and saw us. They ran toward us. One was Inspector Lestrade, even at this hour here in person, and I heard his familiar voice as he spoke. "My goodness, Mr. Holmes, Dr. Watson, what has been going on? What a state you are in, we must get help, but what have you been doing?"

Before we could say anything, I heard Mycroft Holmes, who spoke directly to his brother, ignoring Lestrade. "Where are the papers?" he asked, quietly but with authority.

"Colonel Moran has them," replied Holmes brokenly. We saw that he was at the end of his strength, but he continued, "He is to get them to 'Pierrot' by morning…..then Pierrot will at once leave the country".

Mycroft said no more, but turned on his heel and went at once to his waiting carriage. Inspector Lestrade looked on, irritated and a little annoyed, muttering, "Please can someone tell me what this is all about? Who is Pierrot? Is this some kind of game?"

But Holmes heard no more. I felt how his grip on my arm suddenly relaxed, and how he let my waist and arm free. The efforts of this last hour had taken their toll, and now that his duty was done, he collapsed. As he no longer supported me, I fell beside him, and the last that I heard, before a benevolent sleep enveloped me, was the voice of Inspector Lestrade, calling for stretcher-bearers.

Conclusion

As I awoke, I became aware, to my great surprise, that I was in my bed at home. I turned my head and recognised my dear wife, Mary, on a chair beside the bed. She sat with hands folded, and her eyes closed. Her head, bowed over her breast, rose and fell with her slow and regular breathing. Clearly she was sleeping. But I still doubted. Was it real? After the experiences in the Museum, I felt that nothing more could be certain.

"Mary," I croaked, with a voice I hardly recognised. I saw how my dear wife sat up suddenly, and lifted her head to look at me anxiously.

"Mary, is it really you?" I asked, a little steadier, and tried to sit up to stretch my right hand out to her. Her lips moved silently to smile, and tears rolled down her face, tears of relief and happiness. Then she leaned over, took me in her arms and stroked my forehead. She could not speak, but there was no need. As I felt her warmth, in my arms, I knew that it was reality, I was indeed home again.

When I fell back on the pillow, exhausted by this gentlest of welcomes, Mary began to explain that it was Holmes' doing, that I was here with her at home in Kensington. As I gathered strength to ask her what had happened, she explained what she knew.

First of all, Inspector Lestrade had arranged to have Holmes and myself admitted at once in hospital. As Holmes came round on the Monday afternoon, he was determined to discharge himself. Then he asked about me, and my condition, and was told that apart from the concussion, I appeared to have no further injuries. The doctors had said that I should have absolute quiet, and remain confined to bed. Holmes had immediately insisted that I would then be better off at home, with my wife to look after me. The doctors naturally resisted, properly fearful of complications which could arise. Holmes had insisted, however, that Dr. Smythe, our neighbour, would supervise me, and finally they had allowed me to be transported home by ambulance wagon, home to Mary, on Monday evening.

Mary paused in her account, and I caught something in her words about which I had to ask.

"Mary, if that was Monday evening as you said, what day is it now?"

"Today is Wednesday, John, Wednesday, the 6th of August. You slept more than forty-eight hours, my dear. I had already been very worried, whether that was normal, and asked Dr. Smythe to examine you again. His opinion was that you were recovering normally, that all was well and that sleep and calm were the best medicines for you."

I felt that this conversation had already demanded too much of my strength. And yet there was so much that I needed to know. The overpowering desire to close my eyes and sleep again, however, was too much. There was still one question I had to ask Mary,

"Do you know how Holmes is?"

"When they brought you home, I saw him, because he insisted, apparently against all the rules, in being with you in the ambulance. He was very pale, and his hands were grotesque, as they were bound up to heal from the damage they had suffered. Even so, he seemed to be in good spirits. I suspect that it had done him good to argue at the hospital and to pitch his stubborn head against the experts, for he seemed to be pleased as he spoke with me about it".

I had to smile as I thought of the discussion. His performance at the hospital was perhaps out of order, but it corresponded perfectly to my friend. Curiously, it reassured me, so that I could close my eyes and sleep again.

I will not tire you, dear reader, with a description of my recovery. It is enough when I reassure you that Mary looked after me. In my few waking hours during the daytime, she ensured that I at least consumed enough to keep up my strength, and she read to me, but only from lighter works. Apart from Dr. Smythe she allowed no-one to visit me, and she also kept the newspapers away from me. She just once allowed a message from Holmes to be sent to me, in which he told me, in the hope that I was progressing well, that, when I felt sufficiently recovered, he would appreciate my visit.

Some ten days later, when I felt well enough, and with Dr. Smythe's approval, I could take up Holmes' invitation. The morning of Wednesday, August 13th, I spent again in my practice, and then, in the afternoon, went to visit Holmes.

Once more in Baker Street at 221B, I first met Mrs. Hudson, who of course wanted to know all about my condition. I then took the stairs, and went up to our old shared apartment. Knocking first, I heard Holmes call "Come in," and the door opened. He sat in his favourite chair, staring into the fireplace. He turned to look at me, but it was clear that he was occupied with his thoughts, and realised only after a moment's reflection, that I was there. Suddenly his eyes lit up, and a smile broke out on his face. He jumped up and came to me, to seize my hand and shake it warmly.

"Watson, old friend, how are you now?"

I recited to him how well I had recovered, and asked him in return. "Wonderful, Watson, even my hands seem as good as new. It was very hard, not being able to use them for days on end".

As he said this, he showed me his hands, which I had last seen torn and bleeding, and I could satisfy myself that they were well healed. There was little to betray the torture he had imposed upon them. I said so, and then asked him what been the outcome of this whole affair, which we had just pursued with such intensity. He gave me a satisfied smile. We took up our accustomed places by the fireplace, poured out two whiskies, and Holmes began to tell me.

"I think, Watson, you know most of the facts, but there are some elements of which you were not aware,"

"Quite so, Holmes, especially since I know nothing from the moment when Lestrade and your brother Mycroft came up to us. Moreover, Mary had deliberately kept away from me all news and controversy. I only know that it was thanks to you that my convalescence was at home, instead of in hospital."

Holmes grinned at me as he recalled the episode. He then began thoughtfully to stuff his pipe as he looked at me, and suggested, "Perhaps it will be best if you address to me your own questions."

"A good idea, Holmes, as I must first know whether the man 'Pierrot' succeeded in getting the papers out of the country. And then I would like to know who it is who hides behind this name."

"First of all, Watson, I can reassure you. The papers never left London. Indeed, as I understand, they are now in a safe in Buckingham Palace itself. What they are doing there we do not need to know. With Mycroft's lead, several agents of Her Majesty's services were able to follow Pierrot to Charing Cross Station, where he had intended to board the Continental Express, and relieve him of the papers just as he was buying a travel ticket. He will not have noticed the loss until he was on the train, or indeed already on the continent, He can however scarcely complain that he had been robbed, when the lost material was itself already stolen and he had no right to have it in his possession.

And your second question, referring to Pierrot, he is a secret agent of the Imperial German government, whom our authorities been observing for some time. He has been living at 13 Caulfield Gardens, in Kensington, and works mainly in London. His real name is Hugo Oberstein, and although he is young, he is already quite well-established. Had Mycroft and his agents suspected that the missing Suez papers were coming to London, they might have arranged special observation of Pierrot. You may know that there are many small fish in this business, with all sorts of interests, but there are very few who would have been entrusted with such an important affair".

As Holmes concluded, he looked at me for the next question.

"What did you write in the note that Mrs. Hudson had to take to Mycroft?"

Oh, that was just to explain the situation to Mycroft, and to ensure that he could respond. I believe I wrote, "Can perhaps recover Suez Canal papers. Come to British Museum at once, bring support."

"It is then no wonder that he responded so quickly. I have really no more questions on the secret papers. But there is one question: Holmes, how did you know where to look in the Mummy?"

"Ah, you may recall, I ran my hands over the Mummy first, and then, with the help of the lantern, looked for something striking."

"Yes, I recall that. And was there anything striking?"

"There certainly was, Watson. The place which I opened was the same that Dr. Miller had used. After he had opened the mummy, and inserted the papers, he closed the cut with a piece of gauze, and with glue. That had naturally neither the consistency nor the feeling of the original material, and so I was able to find it quite easily."

"Now, Holmes, I can understand how you could cut into the Mummy so easily with your pocket-knife, and open it."

My friend nodded his agreement. Carrying on from this, I asked, "And what has become of Brian Hammond?" He smiled before answering me.

"He has for the last week been a free man".

I looked at Holmes in disbelief. How could that have happened so quickly? It had surely been impossible to bring charges before a court. It would have meant, in three days, preparing charges, bringing evidence, including that which would exonerate the accused, and arriving at a verdict. Holmes obviously followed my thought, because he immediately explained that a charge had never been placed.

"Scotland Yard, represented by our friend, Inspector Lestrade, reported that his enquiries had brought important evidence showing that Brian Hammond could at once be released from custody. When questions were asked about the nature of this evidence, Lestrade blocked them by saying that ongoing investigations made it impossible for him to reveal details.

'The Times' published a lengthy article in which the innocence of Mr Hammond was made clear, and endorsing his good reputation, which had been unjustly put in question by recent events".

"It would be interesting to know what new evidence was available," I suggested.

"You will not learn that, Watson, for there was no such evidence."

He smiled and continued, "New evidence is only a technical turn of speech, to conceal that considerable pressure was brought to bear to achieve his release. My brother had recovered the secret papers, and was anxious to thank me in a practical way. I told him that the best expression of these thanks would be to ensure Brian Hammond's immediate release."

"But Holmes, you could certainly have cleared him before a court and jury?"

"Indeed, Watson, but I would have had to involve the story of the two miniatures, which, even if they saved him from the rope, would have been most harmful to his good name."

I had to agree. My next question was then, "But what about Professor Hammond, have you told him the truth about his nephew?"

"No, Watson, I have not. Both the Professor and Brian were here to thank me, but I had instructed Mrs. Hudson not to receive them. She had to plead that my state of health did not yet admit of my receiving visitors. We therefore made an appointment for August 13th."

"Why, Holmes, that is today."

"Quite so, Watson, and when you knocked and entered, I was a little confused, as I was expecting them".

"But why did you leave it so long?" I had to ask.

Holmes answered thoughtfully, "I wanted to give Brian Hammond at least a week to reflect upon everything. I hope now that the young man has indeed done so. If, as I believe, he is truly a young gentleman, he will by now have told his uncle what had really happened".

"Holmes, when we speak of protecting a good reputation, I must think also of Dr. Miller. What has happened there?"

"I can reassure you that we need to have no anxiety in that respect, Watson. Dr. Miller's gaming debts, and the connection which resulted to the organisation of Professor Moriarty, are so closely connected to the theft of the secret papers, that not a word will be said in public. Nothing will be made known."

I was most relieved to hear this. I was particularly concerned that Mrs. Miller, with her as yet unborn child, should not have to suffer the shame of her late husband's errors. Her life as a young widow and mother would be difficult enough. I reflected for a moment, but then came upon another thought. It troubled me.

"And what will happen to Colonel Moran? Has he been arrested, and will he be charged for attempted murder?"

"No, Watson, he has not."

I was very surprised, and burst out, "But Holmes, this man would have killed us both! Surely he must be held to account for what he has done! You must have told Lestrade what happened in the cellars of the British Museum! If not, I would go to tell him myself."

"Good old Watson, yes, I know, always ready to act. Naturally I spoke with Lestrade. I have told him as far as discretion allowed, what we were doing in the museum. I told him how we saw that a band had broken in, and that we wanted to prevent anything worse. I said that we were overpowered, and that Colonel Moran and his men had shut us in the burning cellar."

Holmes paused and busied himself again with his pipe.

I was so impatient that I asked again, "But what did Lestrade do?"

"He went to the 'Bar of Gold,' ready to arrest Colonel Moran on charges of breaking and entering, of attempted murder, and arson. What he obtained, was some twenty sworn statements, that the Colonel had spent the whole evening gambling in the club, and had never left it."

I was very shocked, and looked at him as I burst out in indignation, "Admitting that twenty statements might sound convincing, I would seriously question what sort of doubtful individuals had given them. Our evidence is surely above reproach."

Holmes permitted himself a bitter, almost cynical smile. Then he said, "Watson, I might have thought as you do, but Lestrade showed me a list of the sworn statements, and you would not wish to know who stood behind them. Do not imagine that such corruption is a privilege of the lower orders. There were so many supposedly honourable persons there, who are prominent in society, persons whose names are their guarantee, whose word would be taken as absolutely beyond question. Compared to them we count for little, indeed, no more than dust under their shoes. No, Watson, to make allegations against Colonel Moran serves in these circumstances little purpose. I fear we would more likely end up with a charge of libel."

As I looked at Holmes, bitter and disappointed, I saw that he felt just as I did.

"And what about Professor Moriarty?" I asked, almost resigned to the thought that I already knew the answer.

My friend drew on his briar pipe before answering. "There is, as we might have expected, not the slightest indication which might connect him with the whole affair."

Thinking on Holmes' last words, we sat for a while silently, side by side, each lost in his own thoughts. I noticed that each of us was suffering under the thoughts that this outcome provoked. I decided to ask again, "Holmes, did the fire in the cellar do much damage?"

"It appears that around the half of the material stored there might have been lost. The fire could however be prevented from reaching the ground floor or other parts of the building. The watchmen, who had been bound and gagged by the gang, could all be saved. We might therefore conclude that the damage was not as severe as might have been the case."

"I fear that Lord Armstrong, the Museum Director, may not see it in that light," I remarked, and I saw how Holmes nodded his agreement.

At that moment we heard the house bell being rung. Holmes looked up and said, "That will perhaps be Professor Hammond and his nephew."

Within moments, there was a knock on our door, my friend called to come in, and as the door was opened, Mrs. Hudson showed in the two Hammonds. They greeted us and at once thanked Holmes and myself for our efforts in the case. I found myself wondering whether Holmes would bring up the matter of the miniatures from the museum. There was however no need; Professor Hammond spoke of the theme himself.

"I really must most earnestly thank you, that you have protected the good name of my nephew. As soon as Brian was released, he told me the truth about the whole story, and at first I was very angry and ashamed. After reflecting on the whole affair, however, and of the ordeal to which he had been submitted, I decided that he deserved a second chance. He has, as I am now sure, learned from his mistakes. That is surely the most important outcome."

"That, Professor Hammond, is just how I feel about it," said Holmes. Professor Hammond wanted to ask Holmes about his fee for conducting his enquiries. Holmes was able to convince him, however, that Brian's innocence was really a matter which had been resolved in the course of a quite different affair, for which payment had already been settled. Both Hammonds thanked Holmes profusely, and with this the interview was at an end. They prepared to leave the apartment, but before they did, Holmes called Brian Hammond and addressed him. "Mr Hammond," he said sternly, "if you would wish to repay my efforts on your behalf, you will now demonstrate, in all that you do, that my opinion of you was justified, and that you have truly deserved another chance."

"I promise you, Mr. Holmes, that I will do everything I can to justify your confidence and the trust you have shown in me," said Brian Hammond. His serious expression broke into a broad smile, as he turned to follow his uncle to where he was already waiting on the ground floor.

A few moments after they had left, Mrs Hudson knocked and opened our door, standing there somewhat expectantly. We looked at her in surprise. "Mr. Holmes, as I saw your visitors out at the front door, I found this on the step."

She gave Holmes a bunch of white long-stem lilies, which were held with a broad black ribbon, tied in a bow. Under the knot there was a black-edged envelope, addressed to Holmes.

"Thank you, Mrs. Hudson," he replied thoughtfully, and took the lilies from her.

Mrs. Hudson looked inquisitively at me, but I could only shrug my shoulders. She went out muttering, "But we have no bereavement here." Holmes opened the envelope and took out a card. As he read what was written, I saw how he raised his eyebrows, and a knowing smile came to his lips.

"A few friendly lines from Professor Moriarty, Watson. Would you like to read them?" I took the card and could hardly believe what I saw.

I am pleased that I must not yet lay this wreath on your grave. It is most rewarding to measure my intellect against yours. I would, however, urgently advise you, in the interests of your well-being, to refrain in the future from such activities.

"But Holmes, that is nothing but a direct threat," I had to say. My friend nodded wisely over my observation. "What are you thinking to do about it, Holmes?"

"I will not allow myself to be diverted from my task. I will continue exactly as before. One day, Watson, there will be a final confrontation between me and Moriarty. Indeed, in order to defeat this Napoleon of crime, I am quite ready to sacrifice my own life."

As he said this, he looked out into the empty distance. He did not at once notice, how much his words had disturbed me.

"My dear old friend, do not let yourself be so troubled! It is not yet at that point. And be reassured, that I do not intend to sacrifice myself without a struggle. But we will waste no more time with such morbid thoughts".

He made a quick movement, and the lilies were in the back of the fireplace, where they were rapidly consumed in bright red flames.

"Now, Watson, what do you say to dinner at Simpson's. Have you time for me? If you would like to come with me, we can after dinner hear Sarasate play in St. James' Hall."

"I would be pleased to join you", I said truthfully. "As I left home, Mary wished me an agreeable evening, and I had warned her that it might be late. She will not wait for me, as she needs the rest after the burden of caring for me in these last days."

"Then, Watson, we may enjoy an agreeable evening together. Allow me a few moments to exchange my housecoat for more suitable dress." He disappeared into his bedroom, and reappeared ready to go out.

I had however something on my mind, which I had to share with him.

"Holmes," I began, a little hesitantly. He looked at me, as always aware of the way my thoughts were disturbing me.

"Holmes, I have to thank you most sincerely. You saved my life in that cellar. I still have the feeling that I was of no great value to you." Ashamed of myself, I looked down at my shoes.

Holmes stood up very straight and said, "My dear friend, as so often, you fully underestimate your own contribution. You are a whetstone on which I can sharpen my own wits. You are always a great help, and I know that I can always rely on you, however great the danger. You will always be there at my side. I have also not forgotten that, as Colonel Moran fired his revolver, you pulled me out of his firing line; and it was your selfless search for the block and tackle which gave us the means whereby we, in fact, escaped from the cellar. As for saving you, I know that if the roles were reversed, you would just as naturally have given up yourself to save me."

His obviously sincere words left me glowing with relief. I smiled at him, and he too relaxed. He then, with deliberately theatrical tone, continued, "And now Watson, you really should learn, in future, just when we are about to go out, not to begin on some theme which will bring us to Simpson's too late to find a table!"

He laughed, took up his hat and stick, and set off down the stairs. I followed as best I could.

His vigour had thus, at least for this evening, swept away all my worries about Professor Moriarty and Colonel Moran. After the events of these last few weeks, I was sure that he could now enjoy a somewhat quieter time. How could I then know that it would be through me that Holmes would soon find himself called to investigate the circumstances of a mysterious death on the Continent?

End

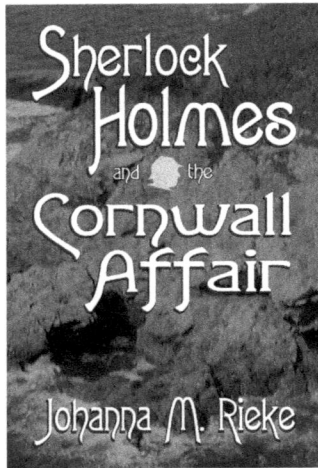

Do you love Cornwall, with its cliffs and breakers, sleepy fishing harbours and villages? Would you like to meet a real English Lord? And do you enjoy an authentic, well researched historical crime story? With the author you will accompany the renowned Baker Street detective, Sherlock Holmes, and his friend Dr Watson, on their journey to Cornwall. There, in idyllic surroundings, they are faced with seemingly impenetrable questions, leading to desperate villainy. A fifty-year-old history of intrigue, smuggling, betrayal, murder and revenge waits to be revealed, and you are there, with Holmes and Watson.

Also from Johanna M. Rieke

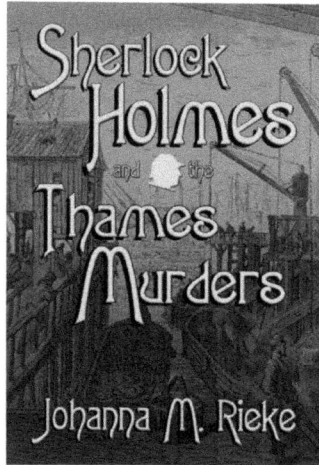

London in 1890 is shocked by a series of gruesome murders. There seems to be no rhyme or reason to them, except for their location in the Thames dockland. Scotland Yard is perplexed. Can Sherlock Holmes and Dr Watson help before worse follows? And what is really going on? Author Johanna Rieke brings rich and poor in Victorian London realistically to life, as she unfolds for you the surprising story of the Thames Murders, as disaster is averted at the last moment.

Also from Johanna M. Rieke

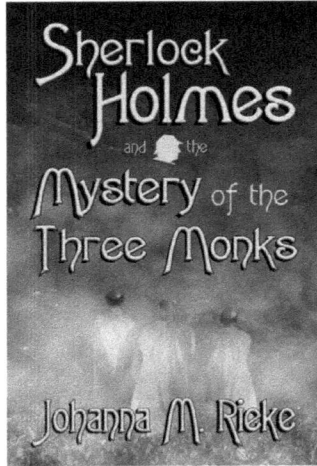

It is summer in 1890, in Robertsbridge, a small village in East Sussex. Dr Watson, on holiday without Holmes, finds the village peaceful and sleepy, but the truth is different. He soon discovers that the villagers are afraid, the atmosphere is threatening. Why do three mysterious white monks haunt the ruined abbey? What does the gipsy seek? Where is a missing ten-year-old boy? Watson calls for Holmes, but why is Holmes fearful of endangering lives? We read in this exciting story how Holmes' patient deduction and Watson's courage come together, to solve a many-sided mystery just before it turns into disaster.

MX Publishing

MX Publishing brings the best in new Sherlock Holmes novels, biographies, graphic novels and short story collections every month. With over 400 books it's the largest catalogue of new Sherlock Holmes books in the world.

We have over one hundred and fifty Holmes authors. The majority of our authors write new Holmes fiction - in all genres from very traditional pastiches through to modern novels, fantasy, crossover, children's books and humour.

In Holmes biography we have award winning historians including Alistair Duncan, Paul R Spiring, and Brian W Pugh

MX Publishing also has one of the largest communities of Holmes fans on Facebook and Twitter under @mxpublishing.

www.mxpublishing.com

Also from MX Publishing

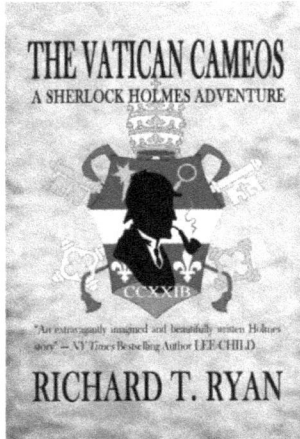

When the papal apartments are burgled in 1901, Sherlock Holmes is summoned to Rome by Pope Leo XII. After learning from the pontiff that several priceless cameos that could prove compromising to the church, and perhaps determine the future of the newly unified Italy, have been stolen, Holmes is asked to recover them. In a parallel story, Michelangelo, the toast of Rome in 1501 after the unveiling of his Pieta, is commissioned by Pope Alexander VI, the last of the Borgia pontiffs, with creating the cameos that will bedevil Holmes and the papacy four centuries later. For fans of Conan Doyle's immortal detective, the game is always afoot. However, the great detective has never encountered an adversary quite like the one with whom he crosses swords in "The Vatican Cameos."

"An extravagantly imagined and beautifully written Holmes story"
(**Lee Child**, NY Times Bestselling author, Jack Reacher series)

Lightning Source UK Ltd.
Milton Keynes UK
UKHW020657281021
392934UK00007B/113